An Affair of the Heart

for my father, with love

An Affair of the Heart

Clare Morgan

Seren is the book imprint of
Poetry Wales Press Ltd,
4 Derwen Road, Bridgend, Wales, CF31 1LH

www.serenbooks.com
facebook.com/SerenBooks
Twitter: @SerenBooks

ISBN: 9781851111746
Ebook: 9781781726921

A CIP record for this title is available from the British Library.

The publisher acknowledges the financial assistance
of the Books Council of Wales.

Cover artwork: 'Bathodyn Calon' by Meirion Ginsberg.
Photograph courtesy of the Martin Tinney Gallery.

Printed by Severn, Gloucester

CONTENTS

JACKSON SQUARE

'Hang on a minute,' said Ellie as she closed the door behind her and stepped out onto the tarmacadam forecourt of the Moonrise Motel. A large black woman with pink curlers in her hair said,

'You talking t' me, Honey?' as she just managed to shiver the edges of her bulk out of Ellie's way, light on her tiny feet as some parody of a ballet dancer.

Ellie shook her head and fixed on a smile which lasted a second or two, then ducked behind her dark glasses and walked towards the car.

The neon sign above the orange moon lying on its back flashed 'Adult Movie Included', and directly under the moon, blue dots informed all comers, in a complicated geometric pattern, that the rooms were clean.

'God save me from "Ol N'Awlins",' thought Ellie, kicking aside a piece of trash, but this time she kept the thought entirely within herself, her lips didn't move as they had done a few minutes before, she made a conscious effort to remember she was on her own.

The car looked hot and dusty in the Sunday sunlight, a white hirecar that cost thirty dollars a day plus five dollars collision damage waiver ('these big ol trucks here on the L'isiana highways can kick up a stone t' crack a win' shiel easy as winkin'). She'd deliberately chosen a small, German car. She didn't feel like handling the great big American monstrosities, all chrome and soft suspension, and so long from nose to tail it was just about impossible to find a place to park.

Today she didn't feel like handling the small car either, European and relatively dear to her though it might be. She walked past it and out of the motel parking lot and away from the orange moon lying on its back, out onto Airline Highway where four lanes of cars and trucks hammered and boomed their way down town, towards the distant white concrete fingers of the New Orleans business district, gesticulating like spectral fingers in the creeping heat.

'Which state y'all from?' asked the cab driver without much interest. For once, she had managed to hail a black and white cab. She debated saying 'Mississippi' which usually shut them up, but thought, perhaps it was better to tell the truth, and said, 'England' and listened with a patience born of practice to the exclamations and questions which bred off one another and the man's active tongue like so many maggots off the dirt of a hot day.

Being European in New Orleans was a terrible penance. They hungered after anything the least bit English. They lusted with an effete fascination for the French. Yet at the same time they saw it all from the confident perspective of the New World, where anything was possible and a 'Po-Boy' sandwich was big enough to feed an ordinary human being for a week.

'The Quarter, y' said?'

They had already passed under the overhanging canopies of concrete and were coming among the peeling porches of the Vieux Carré. The man was looking at her doubtfully. She could see his eyes reflected in the driving mirror. She didn't like people looking at her.

'Bourbon Street?' said the man. 'Bienville?'

She nodded, and he swung the big cab up to the kerb, forcing a woman who had just stepped off the sidewalk to step back on again, pursing her lips into an exclamation of annoyance and waving a paper bag on which was printed 'Ma Hennessey's Praw-leens, Best in N' Awlins'.

The cab driver spat through the window. The spittle sizzled a little as it hit the sidewalk and immediately dried. The heat of the Quarter came in through the window and sucked like leeches at the flesh of Ellie's neck.

'Gwine be that kinda day,' said the driver as she gave him a twenty dollar bill.

Ellie said, 'Sure' and tipped him two dollars instead of one, she didn't know why, it was a whimsical thing to do, she was either tired or lonely, or maybe sickening for something, N' Awlins *grippe*, it was generally the *grippe* that made you tip more than you had to.

A lot of the shops in the Rue Royale were shut. A few early tourists were standing outside the polished plate glass of one of the big antique shops and staring in at its rich mahoganys, the banks of crystal chandeliers which made the otherwise dark interior sparkle like a gem-filled den. A few late prostitutes were picking their way up Iberville towards their shuttered rooms at the back of Bourbon. Their spiky heels clacked on the dry sidewalk. Their make-up was melting, and their black, shiny jackets and skin-tight skirts seemed to suck up the heat.

Ellie wondered how many tricks you could turn on a hot night, plying your trade down by the French Markets in the arching shadows of racks and alleyways, with the heavy smell of chicory and sweet beignets coming out of the Café du Monde and winding itself up into your clothes and hair. Maybe it would be strange to sell yourself like that. Maybe it would be good to get paid for all the loveless acts of copulation you sweated and sighed your way through, listening for the gasp and shudder which set you free, feeling the skin cooling, waiting in that startling vacancy which was like a presentiment of your own death.

'*Take pity on a fine young fella from outa town?*'

A shadow fell across her and she was for the moment disoriented by the size and depth of it shutting her off so suddenly from the sun. She blinked and saw a large man standing by her in shiny, sharp-toed boots and a new-looking ten-gallon hat. Across his chest she made out the letters 'TEXAS: THE LONE STAR STATE'. Ellie stared at him for a minute, trying to grasp what it was he wanted. For a minute, she had the idea that he was propositioning her. A whole series of feelings went through her, she experienced them all like little needles stuck into her flesh and deftly turned, sending sensations out to every corner of the territory her flesh covered, like fleet-footed messengers spreading the news up-country of an unexpected declaration of war. But of course, the idea was ridiculous. The man wasn't really standing all that close to her. He was standing several feet away, accosting one of the prostitutes who had passed by on the other side. She didn't hear the prostitute's reply. In a way, she had hardly heard the proposition. It was one of those occasions when there seems to be a space in your head that the words drop into, and you wonder, are they real, and look around trying to locate their source.

The prostitute laughed at something, and walked on. And then the man was right by Ellie, a big man in a too new ten-gallon hat. He didn't say anything, didn't even look at her.

She really had nothing to worry about. Most men knew a respectable woman when they saw one. But Ellie looked at him, she had to look up, he was so tall, and noticed his eyes were a peculiar pale grey, the kind of eyes which are like tunnels you imagine you could travel down to get to the centre of a person's head. Ellie was vaguely afraid of him. They passed each other, and his shadow was heavy as she went through it.

She felt thirsty, but didn't like to go into one of the bars at the corner of Chartres and St Philip. The interiors were dark and cool-looking. The ceiling fans flashed like cool white knives and made a faint whuffing noise you could just hear out in the street. There were only men inside, you could see the blurry outline of men's hips and men's legs, the stretchy melon shapes their buttocks made, straining against the light cotton of their trousers as they got into position over the pool cue. 'Click' went the cue as the tip of it hit the smooth surface of the ball. 'Click' went the ball as it dropped down into the pocket. Ellie licked her lips because her mouth was dry and thought how odd it was to see people's teeth so white and disembodied against the black background, like the last mortal relic of somebody who is about to become a ghost.

There were more people about as she headed slowly down Decatur towards the river. As she passed the first of the praline shops and smelt the hot, thick toffee smell which always hung around the doorways, the hollow howl of the steamboat *Natchez* echoed towards her from the wharf. She was really beginning to feel the heat. Her arms and her legs felt sweaty and a damp patch was forming in the scooped out space between her shoulder blades.

'*Take pity on a fine young fella?*'

She turned around quickly but could see neither the man nor his too new hat. She felt suddenly claustrophobic. She thought, I'll go up onto the Moonwalk and sit by the river. The river always had a special kind of effect. It calmed her. Maybe it was the size of the thing, so wide, it must be a mile from here to Algiers Wharf, so long, thousands of miles maybe, coming from the other end of the country and just flowing, flowing, the same way it had done since who knew when.

She climbed the concrete steps and walked along the wooden promenade and watched the tourists watching the muddy waters swerve in against the levee. A man and a woman walked past with their arms around each other. Ellie thought they were probably from New York. They looked as if they came from New York. They were quite young and looked at each other more than they looked at the water. Ellie remembered feeling like that. It seemed a long time ago. The thought of it made her shiver slightly. She walked along the wooden promenade and watched the tourists get down to the edge of the water and stoop to touch the water and straighten up shaking their fingers in mock consternation, and clamber back again. *She* wouldn't go down to touch the water. You wouldn't catch her doing that. Not likely. Not with the chemical works one on top of the other all the way up both banks, right up as far as Baton Rouge, and, for all she knew, probably beyond. No, she wouldn't touch the water. You never could tell just what it was filled with. And yet, the thought of the water drew her, so that she went right to the edge of the wooden promenade and stood looking down, watching her own image thick in the brown-grey grains of it ten or so feet below.

She felt very tired. She walked over to one of the benches and sat down and squinted because the sun reflected right off the surface of the water and into her eyes. She couldn't be bothered to open her bag and find her sunglasses. A sense of lethargy sank right down into her. She felt it in her legs, which were so heavy they might have been planted in the promenade, an extension of the bench on which she sat; she felt it in her arms too, and her head, they were dense and heavy, all the pieces seemed set and dense in relation to each other, she might have been inanimate, except for the thoughts which heaved inside her skull, kind of white and shiny and massed like maggots are, when you lift the lid of some dark old jar and peer cautiously in and discover them.

'No no no no nooaw.' The man whose mouth the words came out of was hunched up at one end of the next bench. He was dressed in an old grey jacket which didn't fit him, a shiny jacket which made his hands look bony and big, and a pair of cotton trousers too long in the leg, so they bagged around his ankles and draped like used balloons over the ragged canvas of his down-at-heel sneakers. The man stopped moaning, but Ellie saw at the corners of his mouth little bunches of bubbles which she knew contained more 'noes', every time one burst it let out another silent 'no', and when enough burst and a thin bit of spittle slid down and hung under his chin, that was a 'no' too. Ellie looked away. You often saw down-and-outs on the Moonwalk. They met there, sitting on the wooden seats with their brown paper parcels holding all they had stowed under the seats, and the liquor bottles stuffed in their pockets making them lumpy looking, all lumps and red-rooted eyes. It was strange to see them mixed up with the tourists. Sometimes one of them would come up and ask for a dollar. You knew you had to refuse. You just shook your head. That was enough. You didn't look at them. It was always a mistake to look. You looked – not through them, so much as past them, so they were kept right to the edges of the space that made up your sight. But it was strange how clear they were, all the same. Clear in your memory days after. Like faces in the crowd at Botticelli's Crucifixion. Faces whose expressions you remembered more clearly than the face of the dying Christ.

The *Natchez* was moving out over the water, heading downstream with the water falling off her paddles like the shredded fabric of a greyish veil. Ellie screwed up her eyes and tried to make out the people on the three decks, but she couldn't get them any clearer than matchstick men and women, static black ants. She remembered the last time she had been on the *Natchez*. She had sat with a man, held his hand as the shore drew away from them, felt the warm flesh of his hand and watched the grey water churning underneath the wheel. And thinking about it now, the absence of his hand hurt her. She wondered how it could be that absence was more powerful than presence.

She felt the balance of things altered by this new idea, as though someone were weighting a scales with an illicit thumb. She got up and walked purposefully away from the river, and across the square. A young woman was having herself sketched. Ellie stopped and watched the artist's quick fingers wielding the wild lines of charcoal into the approximation of a face. Something about it made the flesh at the top of her neck get tight, like it did when someone you'd been wanting to, touched you.

She wondered if she might not buy an ice cream, but the shop at the corner of Chartres was full of teenagers taking languid bites out of each other's red-topped Cornettos. She thought, 'I'll just drop into St Louis's', and stepped through the arched doorway into the coolish interior of the Cathedral with a feeling of relief. But you weren't allowed just to look around.

An elderly man with slicked down hair and a check jacket and knife-edge creases in his trousers herded her with a group of middle-aged women into a little corralled-off area, all looped rope and quick release fastenings, and said,

'Now, Dear Ladies, you don't *have* to give a thing. My time here is donated on an entirely voluntary basis – ' Ellie wanted to get away but found herself fitting a dollar into the man's ready hand, dragging her heels along behind the women's endless questions, what was the date of a certain painting, where was the location of the casting of the original bell.

But the light was nice. The way it came in through the stained glass. And the place was peaceful, once the women had spent their allotted fifteen minutes and gone, in a bevy of exclamations, back out into the heat. Ellie sat at the back and watched the light change on the face of a plaster angel. Above her the bell tolled the half hour then the hour. She began to feel conspicuous, no one else just came and sat the way she was sitting, and eventually she went out and bought some prawleens and sat in the grassy enclosure whose iron railings marked the heart of Jackson Square, and shared the afternoon with the trash bins and the birds which zoomed in looking for bits, clicked and picked for a minute, and flew off.

At five or thereabouts it started to feel like evening. The pace of things changed, the street musicians packed up their bad jazz and their instruments and shambled off. The breeze changed direction and blew in now from the interior, redolent at its edges with swamp and bayou bird and the heavily scented petals of some ornamental vine. It was surprising how quickly darkness came down, and how thick it was, despite the individual whitenesses of the lights. The day-people seemed, all of a sudden, to have disappeared, the fat, waddling women from Illinois with paunchy husbands who travelled up-state. The young mothers with fretful children triumphantly riding their fathers' shoulder bones. Oriental couples with up-market dark glasses and discerning fingers pointing out special treasures in posh shops.

All these seemed in the space of a few minutes to have dis-appeared, to have been replaced by the outlines of people, their shadows, the picked out planes of faces – cheek, chin, lip – which shifted and flickered in the interleaved set of reflections that was New Orleans evening.

Ellie would have liked to stay sitting in the little bit of green and feeling the heat diminish. But she knew it wasn't wise. A woman out on her own after dark was asking for trouble. So she got up and walked diagonally over the piece of green, and the flowers in the dusty ornamental border shook their shadowy heads at her, and the smell of the horse dung as she came out past the line of hire carriages was acrid in her nose.

She crossed the road and walked towards the French Markets where she knew she could easily get a cab. In a way it hardly surprised her when the man stepped out of the shadows and said, quite quietly this time,

'*Take pity –?*'

He was a tall man, and she could see in the street light, or maybe it was the subtler light of the rising moon, his shiny, sharp-toed boots and the crisp silhouette of his hat.

From way over on Bourbon Street the strains of a blues tune drifted in. Across the road a young girl laughed and the sound of it tinkled in the gutter like shards of glass. The *Natchez* gave a low moan as it eased out into mid stream.

And before she thought too much about it, Ellie said 'Yes,' and the man grasped her arm, and she liked the way his fingers felt, testing her flesh.

An Affair of the Heart

'Very well,' Maddy said to Jean-Claude that morning when they got up and Paris was grey-looking, and the spindly pointed part of La Tour Eiffel disappeared into the mist, and a wind blew down Rue Royale which seemed to take all the heat out of things and suck it up into that vortex stationed (only the gods knew why) directly over La Place de la Concorde.

'Very well. Perhaps it would be better.'

'Perhaps,' said Jean-Claude looking sideways into his coffee and listening, with only half his attention, to whatever Maddy said. Maddy was much older than Jean-Claude. Nevertheless, she looked comparatively young.

Jean-Claude said, 'I suppose we will do whatever you think best.'

Because she was so much older they usually did what Maddy thought best. It didn't always seem like this. But if one looked at things closely one found it was usually so.

Maddy was fair and aquiline – Jean-Claude had brown hair, and a mouth that was neither one thing nor the other, and he wore small round spectacles with rims. At least, they were almost round, it would be truer to say they were oval, but they were certainly small and were, to Jean-Claude's lasting pleasure, in the very latest fashion. He had left university several years before and had not got on as well as had been expected. As the years passed fashion, therefore, became more and more important to him. Maddy was rather fashionable. To be seen with her gave him a sense of being *au courant*. He had first slept with her about a year before the morning in question. During these twelve months he had had several lovers. But he had no desire to separate from Maddy. She was exciting, and said, when he lay with her arms around him and his face turned in her surprisingly granular breasts, things that no other woman had said to him, not yet in all events, and he was twenty-seven now, no longer the innocent he had once been, and beginning (he admitted it sometimes) to lose hope.

'It won't be too difficult,' she said, her voice taking on that nasal quality which was like a wire pulled in him, going through his bones.

'It's not as if we have, for example, finances in common.'

Jean-Claude put down his coffee and looked at Maddy, who had paused in the act of lifting a piece of buttered croissant to her lips. He thought, can Maddy possibly mean she is leaving me? But why? Has something happened between us that I have forgotten about? He felt confused and tired and didn't want to go on talking but understood that he must.

He said,

'Ah, Maddy – ' and made his voice go calm at the end, in that soft way he had that Maddy liked, particularly when he was talking about love, which he wasn't now because it would have been inappropriate, but which he hoped to be able to come around to, not immediately but in a little while, that was how one had to be with women, always coming around to things indirectly, using soft words where hard ones would have been appropriate, kissing and touching them oh so gently, when what you really wanted was a quick fuck.

Maddy put the croissant into her mouth and chewed it, and Jean-Claude was fascinated for a moment by the circular way her jaw went, round round round, and her eyes, above that movement, still and unblinking, depthless but insurmountably deep, yellow and green and speckled and enclosed, the coloured bit, in a hazy-looking ring.

She said,

'No, Jean-Claude,' and put her hand flat on the table and before he realized quite what she was doing had got up and gone from him, and all that was left of her in any immediate way was the empty cup and the crumbs and the sideways knife and the crumpled up napkin, all so confounding, so much more 'Maddy' than the presence in the bedroom of which there came intermittent evidence, the hesitation of a drawer opening and closing, the snap of a bottle placed on the dressing table, the sighing sound of the quilt as she pulled it out into the habitual taut shape that she and she alone felt was necessary.

'No, Jean-Claude,' she said again and shook her head in a very decided way as she came past him carrying a handbag and dressed now; she had (it was one of the things that was so attractive about her) been totally naked before. And then, before he knew it she had gone, leaving behind the slight but definite statement her scent made, and a space in his senses, which, had he but known it, nothing and nobody else, in all the time between that morning and the day of his death, which did not happen until he was very old indeed, would fill.

But he knew nothing, that morning we are talking about, that morning built of words and of silences, of pauses and commencements and reiterations and half-articulated hopes and wholly unarticulated globules of despair. It does not matter, but the morning was a morning in May. It does not matter, but May also was the month in which Jean-Claude died (so very many years later). It does not matter, it is just one of life's unfathomable coincidences. And the only people who have any interest in coincidences are those who are very happy or those who are very sad. For most of us, existing in between, coincidence is just a punctuation point.

Jean-Claude did not articulate it thus to himself. He was not, fortunately, an intellectual. And being unaware of his death lying in wait for him already in that distant May, the hottest May of the century and one of numberless blossoms, pink and white and all hues softly indeterminate between, he thought not of coincidence, but of *ennui* and of disharmony, of spirits rubbed one against another, of the soreness of things, but in such a little way really, like in the pattern decreed (perhaps) by a passionless heaven; great though in the schemes of a man who must shave and dress and go forth into the streets of Paris and decide.

That is what Jean-Claude did. He shaved and dressed and went forth into the streets of Paris, and going out among the people was a shock to him, and the roar of the traffic beat against him, assaulted the closed-up sides of his mind, and he didn't notice (which was unusual for him) the pretty girls as they went past him, swinging their bottoms from one side to the other and bending their knees, and looking at him, quite often, through the fringe of their blinking lashes, because he was, if one were to judge him dispassionately, rather a handsome man.

He usually thought of himself as handsome and it gave him pleasure, but today the thought did not occur to him. Maddy was leaving him, yes that must be what she had meant, they hadn't been getting on well recently, and her mouth was closed up very tight, he noticed, when she left. But it was impossible to think of tomorrow without Maddy.

He caught the metro and got off at Varennes by mistake, he'd wanted Invalides, that was the kind of mistake you made when your mind was on other things. He gave two francs to the man who was begging at the top of the steps. He wished, later, that he'd given the two francs to the musician fifty metres further on. But then again, perhaps it was better to beg quietly, there was a certain dignity at least in that, and the musician had been playing out of tune.

Jean-Claude emerged onto the street again and found it was raining. He went to the Musée Rodin and spent a long time standing in front of *Le Baiser* (*Le Penseur* was temporarily at Varennes station, it looked so odd in its glass box with the rush-hour crowds going by, but in a way not at all out of place, more significant, really, than when it was in the museum and people stood before it and looked at it and said 'Ah' and passed on, wondering how soon they could suggest coffee, without seeming unduly *terre à terre*). He was unsure whether Rodin understood women. He was unsure, that day, whether he understood women. Women were like mirrors. Women absorbed and gave back one's attitudes. They were frightening. How stiff the man's back was in *Le Baiser*, and his toes were tensed. How soft the woman looked, and self-forgiving. The man looked as though he were about to fall. And poor Camille Claudel – well, one never knew, that was the way things happened. How odd though, Rodin, and kissing (the night before he had kissed Maddy, and the soft stuff of her belly had moulded itself over his hip).

Oh yes, it was a strange thing, he thought, coming out of the Rodin into the sunshine; it had decided to be sunny for a few minutes in between the rain.

'Well, you can laugh, now I really *do* look like somebody's Nanny,' Maddy said, putting on her glasses and starting the car that night they met, more than a year ago, and he had thought how long her body was, and how he wanted to lie down with her, and stroke the side of her thigh.

And when I get back to the apartment perhaps she will be gone.

He sat in a café under an awning while the rain came down and made plopping noises on the canvas and on the paving stones where the sparrows bobbed about looking for crumbs. The thought was like a door opening. It was like stepping into the *mise en scène* of a half-finished canvas. It was like crossing a desert, the first part, when you start out. It was like becoming the next character in a book which is still being written. It was like being inside oneself and outside at the same time and not knowing what to do about either. (But then a very pretty young woman came and sat at the next table and he thought, looking at the way her arm pressed into the rather generous curvature of the side of her breast, that he would like to sleep with her.)

Perhaps Maddy will be gone.

There was a certain terror in it and a certain joy. He did not understand the nature of the joy but felt it as a kind of excitement. Maddy gone. But that was impossible because he *was* Maddy. Or perhaps it would be truer to say that Maddy was a puppet operated by strings which had their origin somewhere in the dark parts of his heart. Or of his mind, maybe. See: this thought comes and here is Maddy, stopping to put up her umbrella in front of the shoe shop next to the little alley that leads to Le Récamier. Here is Maddy stepping in between the puddles while the water kicks off the tips of her black high heels and spatters the backs of her legs, that part where the leg narrows and becomes, without one realizing it, the ankle. Maddy had such fine ankles, all bone and fragile tendon, and the flesh dipped into a hollow between bone and tendon in which Jean-Claude liked, when they were in bed sometimes, to rest the bulb of his thumb. And now Maddy, hurrying across the street and frowning, perhaps she has forgotten something, perhaps she is late. Her coat is open and a silk scarf hangs loosely around her neck and the ends of it flutter out from under her coat. A man turns to look at her. What can one feel but pride? Pride in one's own special creation.

But there was a Maddy before I met her, thought Jean-Claude, and if that is so, which it is, then there may be a Maddy in the future who exists entirely outside my life.

But this was a thought that could not be allowed to gain ground. That way lay terror, and Jean-Claude was afraid of terror, terror had you cowering in a corner, even when you were smiling and walking along the street; terror woke you in the middle of the night, or the bell of St Merri striking three, it was all the same, that full-bodied sonority which made everything get tight, until you couldn't stand it any more, you were going to vomit, you had to, and rushed to the bathroom and put on the light and were paralyzed for a moment by the brightness, everything so white and there, and you realized you weren't going to vomit, it was all in your head somehow, and you leaned your forehead on the mirror over the basin, and put the palms of your hands flat on it, and murmured something, perhaps it was a plea for forgiveness, and put yourself for the instant at the mercy of the mirror, as though it were an old and trusted friend.

The trouble was, things got out of control. If Maddy left him, she would go to bed with someone else. He didn't like to think of that. But of course he did like to think of it too, he was a man after all, it was not his fault that the vision of one's woman being fucked combined, in an almost magical fashion, an intensity of pain and pleasure that nothing else that happened in one's life could rival.

Maddy being fucked. He'd thought about it once, thought about suggesting it, but that had been in the early days, a month or two after they met, and Maddy had not yet entirely become part of his mind. She had guessed something of what he was thinking and had sat back against the big square pillows, two of them together so she sat rather upright and the flesh where her thigh turned into her hip folded over on itself in an acute angle, she had sat back and smiled at him and said, 'Poor Jean-Claude' and a sense of shame had gradually spread out in him, and with it a sense of fury more overwhelming than any he had felt since as a small boy of three or four (at the most) his mother had come upon him stealing a franc from the pocket of her pinafore so that he could hear it rattle in his brand new money box, which had been a gift, probably for his birthday, and which (due no doubt to an oversight) was still empty a day or two later, and gave him no pleasure when he picked it up and looked at it, for how can there be any pleasure in contemplating that angular darkness, broken by a single slit of light to which nothing offers itself, no glimmer of bronze or silver, no pale crepy-ness such as is exhibited by the well-thumbed edges of a note?

'Poor Jean-Claude.'

He had hated her for at least five minutes, hated the way she took his hand and placed it (with the fingers spread out as wide as possible so that it resembled, in some ways, a great pale claw) on her stomach, which felt lardy and gave way under his fingers, like something with little substance to it, something you encounter sometimes at the far end of a dream.

And since then he had been afraid to think it, pushed it off when it crept up on him, the thought of Maddy naked, *alongée*, someone else's fingers touching her hip (she had such forward hip-bones, very round and womanly, which was odd because she was in some ways rather boyish, or if not boyish exactly, then with an energy which was seldom characteristic of *la femme*).

Somebody walked by whistling. Jean-Claude's coffee had gone cold and he ordered another. He didn't want it, but he needed something to do with his hands. To pick the coffee cup up and put it down again gave him a sense of permanence. It was an action which always comforted him, even many years later, when he was so old that the cup seemed heavy and the distance to the saucer fraught with peril. He thought,

'I should say something to Maddy.'

But what can one person say to another? Sometimes when he lay beside her, hardly ever, once, or at the most twice, he had thought that one day she would die, and the thought had frightened him. But then, the next morning or perhaps it was an hour later, Maddy was up and the light was on and he saw how she was, her buttocks whitish and disfigured, even at their fullest part, by silvery lines in which there was a certain shading, more than a hint of grey. Oh yes, he was certain at such times, in the space between one second and another, that he loved her.

But nothing (he had first realized five years before, when he was passionately in love with a dancer whose name was Gisela, so much in love with her that he could think of nothing else, how her eyes were, the grace with which she disposed her body and her hands, until one day he looked up as she was coming out of the bathroom, they had spent the night together in an hotel bedroom and she had gone to wash, the night together had been particularly satisfactory and a certain messiness had unavoidably accrued, and saw that she was an ordinary woman with breasts that were already somewhat elongated, a woman who smiled too much in bed and breathed his name at inappropriate moments) – nothing, he realized with a final sense of chagrin, stayed the same.

So perhaps it was a good thing that Maddy was leaving, if she was leaving, and the more he thought about it, or rather around it, the more convinced he was that this was the case. Life without Maddy. He felt for a moment a huge emptiness, as though the world had been cored like an apple. He felt some far breath from the end of the universe cooling the warm film of his skin. And then he felt, almost at the same time but not quite, an excitement so sudden that it bordered on exhilaration.

But that lasted no more than half a minute, exhilaration needs something to feed it and Jean-Claude had nothing, the dregs of his coffee were cold and it had begun to rain in earnest, and he thought of how it was to be without a woman, lonely, and dream-like, being alone made things feel dream-like, which was in a way a good thing, but in another way bad, because the links between things stopped working, and when that happened one began to be unable to feel.

'Perhaps it is a good thing not to feel,' he thought, signalling the waiter and watching how the waiter tore the little white slip with his teeth, and deftly flicked the coins into the pouch that he wore snug up against his belly and secured with a wide leather belt around his waist. But he knew even as he started walking towards the metro station and the rain trickled through his quite thick hair (it was not until ten years later that he began to go bald, quietly and without drama, his hair merely refusing to grow back, first in this spot then in that, until as the months went by a hairless circle composed itself around his crown, quite small at first then larger and more noticeable, giving him, in a certain light, the rather forlorn appearance of an unfrocked monk), he knew, as the rain trickled through his hair and onto his scalp and he watched the preoccupied faces of the women walking past him under their open umbrellas, rather ghostly-looking in the light the open umbrellas cast, you could tell how they would look when they were very much older and the flesh had syphoned away from their faces and a certain appealing roundness had disappeared entirely from cheekbone and jaw (it was unfortunate but true he said to himself afterwards, one afternoon when he was about fifty, before his big illness, when there was still that within him which flowed towards women, that flowing of the self being the essence of true desire, when he desired women still, and they exerted power over him, before he became an island around which for a while the waters of the world continued to flow, until one day they stopped flowing, which event was commemorated by a paragraph in memoriam inserted by a distant cousin who had not known Jean-Claude well, but who remembered him mostly as a taciturn old man who was, if one had much to do with him, rather a bore – it was unfortunate but true that age showed in women in an unflattering gauntness, as though the bones were pressing against the skin, there was nothing between them, none of the padding youth has, that creates the illusion of immortality), he knew that feeling was not something one could choose or not choose, no, feeling was something one was burdened with, like a weak chest, or a tendency to hernia, something clamped into one's genes at the moment of conception, fixed in the fabric by some passing and malevolent star.

'Ah, Jean-Claude, he is so sensitive,' his mother had crooned when he was a boy of seven or thereabouts, stroking his straight hair which fell, with hardly any affectation, in a tailored cascade over his brow. And his aunt, who was his mother's sister and unmarried, had echoed her sigh and placed her cool hand on his wrist and drawn her finger down the inside of his wrist and into his palm, and he had felt, with an alarm not entirely unalloyed by pleasure, the specialness of the wholly sentient being, as rare then as always and as fugitive, for rarity must protect itself by whatever method and always without counting the cost.

And so it was, twenty years and eight and a half women later (there had been one unsatisfactory attempt at a twelve-year-old who, he ever afterwards assured himself, he had thought at least seventeen) on that wet May morning that was already drawing away into a grey and undistinguished afternoon, Jean-Claude made his way languidly down the steps and into Varennes metro, and suffered the stale smell of a carriage in which someone had surely urinated, and suffered too a fat woman taking up more than her share of the seat, all the time with a certain perverse joy, because this was after all *living*, and he was a man on his way to discovering whether his mistress has left him.

He missed his stop and had to go back and when he came up out of the metro the rain had stopped. The unexpected absence of rain gave things a new harmony. He thought he saw, in that first moment of emergence into the comparative hurly burly of the *dix-septième*, how things fitted together. But of course what he saw was only an illusion brought about by the euphoria of fear. As he climbed the stairs to the apartment he understood that nothing fitted. He unlocked the door to the apartment rather clumsily, making a lot of noise and making the key grind in the lock as he turned it.

Maddy was there, as usual, doing something or other at the escritoire. She was neither beautiful nor ugly. She was neither large nor small, neither elegant nor ungainly. She lifted her hand almost as far as her chin then lowered it again.

The room seemed dimmer than habitually. Jean-Claude said, 'I've been out,' and Maddy nodded rather absently, and said something about dinner, and mutual friends.

And Jean-Claude understood that there were no events in life. Things happened by a kind of magic. A calmness descended on him. All that had been chaotic before seemed ordered and still. Maddy was still his mistress. She would still lie down beside him. He would put his hand on her. Some things were possessed of an inevitability. It was better. He felt as though the sun would come out at any moment and lighten things, but it didn't. The light in the apartment remained the same dull grey.

The afternoon passed quietly with Maddy writing letters at the escritoire and Jean-Claude listening to music. They dined at dusk and talked of ordinary things. Jean-Claude remembered that dinner for a long time afterwards. He thought, once or twice, that it was what he would remember in the instant of illumination that must surely precede death. But it was not so, he died in his sleep, at about four o'clock in the morning, and had been heard to maintain for several years previously that he no longer suffered the inconvenience of dreams.

When the dusk of that day in question was well settled and dense as only May dusks can be dense, Jean-Claude suggested to Maddy that they go to bed. They made love with a certain restrained fervour which boded well for the affair's continuation. A year and a day later, however, Jean-Claude left Maddy for a younger woman. What became of Maddy is uncertain. Jean-Claude's affair with the younger woman, who was very beautiful and soft, so soft to the tips of your fingers when you touched her, did not last long. She sang rather well in the evenings sometimes, her fair hair shown to advantage, as were her eyes, by candlelight.

But that night in May these things were still ahead of them, quite far ahead as they lay together and the sounds of Paris came in, but faintly, through the bedroom window, and Jean-Claude woke at around four o'clock and felt something, perhaps it was a premonition, or merely the silvery way Maddy's body looked there next to him, all silvery in the half light between dawn and darkness, making it seem, for a moment, as though he had seen a ghost.

A DAY IN THE LIFE OF PRINCESS CRYSTAL

Marielle Burick and Jennifer Kilgetty had been friends for ten years.
Marielle had been born in Germany, to a German father and an English mother, and ever since the mother left the father and brought the
daughter to live in England, the daughter had felt set apart. Jennifer
was Irish through and through. She had been born a mile from
Mizen Head, on the very western edge of Ireland, and the pink cliffs
and the wet winds and the rolling hills that were the limit of her childhood's horizon made the girl different from her English compeers.

The girls had not met until they were nearly twenty and embark-
ing on the serious business of becoming women. They met in the
hairdresser's, where Jennifer was getting her rather tawny hair a trim
and Marielle was being given what they both referred to as afterwards
as 'the treatment'. They got to talking and quite liked each other, and
both were conscious of a certain boredom, and they agreed to meet.
When they met again they still liked each other and within a month
they were living together in a small but comfortable house in a
respectable suburb on the northern outskirts of Birmingham.

'It's very *nice* to be independent,' Marielle said, with a hint of the
German still distorting the edges of her English accent; and Jennifer
agreed.

It was the early 1970s and the world was uncertain where it was
going. Marielle gave up wearing miniskirts, but Jennifer clung to them
long after they had gone out of fashion. She justified this by saying,

'Well. I've got good legs, so why shouldn't I show 'em?' Jennifer
was a child of the sexual revolution but only dimly aware of it. She
went to bed with more young men than Marielle did, who said she
kept to herself because she wanted to, but was secretly afraid of going

all the way, and practiced her orgasms with a hand mirror so she could see what her face looked like in the moment of absolute abandon.

They often got drunk, especially on Mondays, and talked about the men they would like to end up with, and exchanged extreme details about the men they already had.

'Well,' Jennifer said, 'not that you can actually call him a man, poor sod! Not with that little dinky thing he's wearin', where the real equipment ought to be. He's the sort who's been going five minutes before you can make up your mind whether he's in there at all.'

Marielle laughed very loudly over her sixth glass of sherry and said,

'Jenny, you're the end!' and they both set about with gusto the spiced concoction that was, within a ring of rice, the mainstay of their diet at that time, and whose pungent aroma drifted out into the garden on the hot summer evenings when they left the windows wide open, and made the whole neighbourhood stink, it was generally agreed by those who had never smelled one, like a Cairo bazaar.

A few months after they moved in together there was an acute shortage of men. They sat gloomily by the gas fire (the September wind that day had seemed particularly chill) and asked each other where their lives were going.

'I mean, I don't *want* to get married,' said Jennifer. Marielle looked doubtful. 'But what else is there?' she said. 'People get married. It's as simple as that. How many single women of fifty are there? God. Just think of it. In a bedsit when you're fifty!'

And Marielle shuddered, and sat up a little straighter in her chair. Jennifer said,

'But most men are awfully *boring*.'

'They're not. They're not really. It's just a question of finding the right one.'

'Or two or three,' said Jenny, her friend's seriousness making her particularly flippant. 'And then when you've found this special man, then you're both going to live happily ever after. Is that it?'

'Yes,' said Marielle. 'That is it.' And she stopped playing with the ends of her hair and stared straight ahead.

'And then, I suppose you're going to be faithful,' said Jenny. 'Both of yuh.'

She thought for a moment that Marielle was going to lose her temper. Marielle had a very hot temper, although you would never have guessed it. But Marielle laughed suddenly and said,

'Well. P'raps not as happily as *that*. I mean, just imagine, in about twenty years time. You and me meeting. With a husband and some nearly grown up kids. I don't believe it. I just can't believe it.'

Jenny said,

'Well, between then and now a lot of things have got to happen.'

And they both refused to address the thought in public, though it was uppermost with them both in private, that just then nothing was happening in their lives.

Marielle met a young man who'd been to Marlborough, was a Surgeon Lieutenant, and had an influential father. She described him as 'very upright'. She sent Jenny a postcard from Margate, where she and the Surgeon Lieutenant had gone for a dirty weekend. It was one of those rude seaside postcards that English people love sending, all tits and arch expressions, and genitalia imperfectly obscured by deckchairs, and Union Jacks fluttering proudly atop improbable ramparts of sand. '*Wonderful weather. Gerry's taken me sailing*' was all the postcard said. In person a few days later she added that Gerry was really very sweet.

'Sweet enough to live with? Sweet enough for ever and ever?' Marielle smiled and said nothing. But she wished that Jenny would stop being such a killjoy. And to her fiancé, as the Surgeon Lieutenant was to become by the following summer, she said that her friend Jenny suffered from sour grapes.

The accusation was not entirely true. It was true that other people's contentment seemed to Jenny incomprehensible. How could people settle for second best? The Surgeon Lieutenant was definitely second best. He had red hair and freckles and always opened doors and stood back to let you go through them. Marielle said his pubes were red too. He referred to women as 'ladies' and told mildly sexist jokes. Jenny had begun to notice such things. Marielle was becoming very conventional. She had tea with the Surgeon Lieutenant's parents and took endless pains beforehand, practicing with a little silver fork.

Marielle got married and Jennifer stood in the hotel car park and waved her away. The three-course turkey dinner sat heavily on her diaphragm. It had been a hot afternoon. She went inside and had another glass of champagne. The Surgeon Lieutenant's brother got her in a corner and told her he was impotent and tried to kiss her and put his hand down her dress. She found Marielle's mother folding the wedding dress in preparation for taking it away.

'It's always best to turn a wedding dress inside out,' Marielle's mother said, 'before you fold it.'

Jennifer agreed and they exchanged assurances of how happy Marielle was going to be, and then they parted, and Jennifer did not see Marielle's mother again. She did see Marielle quite frequently at first. They still got drunk together, but on Fridays instead of Mondays, and less drunk than they used to because the Surgeon Lieutenant disapproved.

Marielle's and Jennifer's relative fortunes reversed themselves several times in the following few years. The Surgeon Lieutenant was invalided out and found it difficult to get a job. Marielle got pregnant and depressed. Jennifer hovered at the edge of everything. She almost fell in love. She was considered by some few *cognoscenti* to be potentially brilliant. She bought a tiny cottage right out in the country and spent most weekends there. It was peaceful. She liked to lie on her back on the grass and consider the relative depth of the sky. It made her feel heady and vaguely afraid. Sometimes she felt that at any second she might become detached from the earth and float off into that heady emptiness. There was so little between oneself and the ultimate. Sometimes the perspective which let her function as she was supposed to function in the daily turning of the world altered, and she could see, as if a mist had cleared, the extreme tenuousness of everything. How easy it would be for the planets not to move in the same relation. How easy for that chaos on which order was the merest crust, to erupt. She thought once of telling Marielle how she felt but could not. When she saw Marielle, less and less often as the years went by, they would try on each other's dresses, almost as they used to, but now Jennifer told Marielle only the things she thought Marielle wanted to hear. They discussed nothing. They exchanged platitudes. Marielle said she was very happy with the ex-Surgeon Lieutenant. Jennifer did not believe her. Jennifer began living with a man, and when the unhappy times came with him, did not mention them to her friend. She was still struck, from time to time, by the dreadful tenuousness of everything. Sometimes she would look at her arms and her hands and say to herself '*One day these will not exist. One day the flesh will drop from the bone and the bone will disintegrate and all this will be nothing.*' At such times she breathed deeply and tried to focus her mind on living things. She became afraid of travelling in lifts.

Shortly after her thirtieth birthday Jennifer went to spend the week-end with Marielle. They had not seen one another for nearly a year. The ex-Surgeon Lieutenant was away at his mother's. Marielle said he went quite frequently, and added that his mother was a paragon. They tried on each other's clothes when the children were in bed, then tried to eat the spiced concoction Marielle had nostalgically re-created, but gave up half way through.

'I suppose we're getting too old for it,' Jennifer said, and Marielle agreed. They drank wine, but stopped after a bottle. Marielle said,

'We tend to prefer quality to quantity these days.'

After the meal they sat with their elbows on the table and talked about old times. In a way, there seemed very little to say. The *do you remembers?* took on, for Jennifer at least, the monotony of a repeated dream. When she remembered it in her head, the past was terribly important. But put into words as it was here, the words here between them with their elbows on the table and the plates with their half eaten food pushed to one side, and the dregs in the wine glasses casting blurred pink patterns on the creamy table cloth – put into words the past was nothing but a corpse, a stiff thing with all the life gone out of it.

'It's not easy to re-create the feelings,' she said.

'No,' said Marielle, and then they suddenly had nothing to say to one another. They were two women sitting on either side of a table, whose lives were entirely separate. Jennifer looked at Marielle and Marielle looked at Jennifer and neither found a way in to the other, both saw just the separate exterior face of the other and had no means of knowing what was beyond. In a way it was as if they had only just met. But the possibilities of ever coming together were now quite lacking.

The silence lengthened out into a specific thing with an awkward shape. Marielle coughed and it sounded abnormally loud. From upstairs one of the children cried out. Marielle went up and Jennifer followed slowly. It was the girl, who had woken in the middle of a bad dream. She was five years old and resembled the ex-Surgeon Lieutenant, but had something of Marielle's look when she cried. Marielle sat on the bed and got out a book and began reading a story. The story was called *A Day in the Life of Princess Crystal*. Marielle read the story very well. She seemed quite absorbed by it, and her fair hair fell forward in a curtain over the side of her face.

'*Once upon a time there was a beautiful Princess whose name was Crystal,*' she began. '*She lived in a small hut in the middle of a huge dark forest. The sun only managed to find its way through the leaves of the huge trees for one day in every hundred years. The rest of the time Princess Crystal who, because she was a Princess remained young and beautiful, admired her own silver reflection in the green gloom ....* '

Jennifer felt superfluous standing in the doorway and decided to go outside. She went downstairs as carefully as she could and walked round to the side of the house and felt the darkness around her and the coolness, and mixed in with the coolness, small warm eddies of air which unwound themselves against her. She looked up at the sky which was lightish from the as yet unrisen moon. She was intensely aware of the depth of everything. The stars were hot and white. Even her bones ached with the weight of how everything felt. She wanted to scream or get away, but she had the weekend to get through. She was good at getting through things. She walked back to the door and listened for Marielle reading the story, half expecting to hear the magic words '*happily ever after*' drifting down from the open window as the light went out. But to her surprise the light was already out and she could hear nothing but the slight tinkling the wind made, sifting the metal fitment on the gate.

A Wreath for Tiago Sanchez

The sun coming in through the pink curtains made a mosaic pattern on the bed.

Sanchez said to his wife Emily,

'You should get up. It's time.' But she lay with her eyes closed, not speaking to him, not moving, her body a series of sculpted curves under the white counterpane.

In a way, she reminded Sanchez of a corpse. He had only ever seen one corpse, his grandmother's, and she had died a long time ago, when he was a child. He remembered seeing her corpse, or rather the shape of it, at the hospital at La Cidadela. Well! But what a strange smell hospitals had! It made you feel creepy. And those long corridors. And then the beds. Angles and shadows and hard metal edges. And his grandmother had said the mattresses were made of rock! His grandmother had been a small woman, rather stout, with white hair and eyes that were still very dark.

'Oh, you don't want to worry. This thing is nothing,' she had said to him before they came to take her. 'If you let things worry you, Tiago, you're likely to die young.'

And so he'd tried not to worry, but just remembered his grandmother especially in his prayers, like his mamma had told him to, but then his grandmother had died after all, and here he was despite worrying still alive, and his grandmother, poor granny, short and stout as she had been, nothing, a few old bones, a skull and a few loose fillings, somewhere in the slowly shifting silt of the cemetery of the Grey Angel, set in the last bend of the river before the river turned its back on the little village of La Braga, and headed straight for the sea.

'Emily,' he said, staring at the ceiling and lying on his back with his arms straight down by his sides, so that the tips of his extended fingers reached almost to his knees. 'Didn't you hear me? I said it's time.'

His wife moved a little, you could hardly call it a movement, it resembled more a spasm which swells and then subsides.

Sanchez sat up and jerked the sheet down so that his wife's face was exposed. She opened one eye and said,

'Ah, Tiago!' in a way that was mournful and accusatory. She had eyes like his grandmother. Many women, he was surprised to find, had such eyes. Sometimes when he really looked at the eyes of the women in the street, their combined darknesses stunned him, he was like a man bemused.

But in other ways Emily did not resemble his grandmother. Emily was much taller and thinner, and young, still young. It had seemed inviting, to acquire a young wife. But now sometimes he wondered. His father had said to him,

'Well, Tiago. You can't go wrong, you know, not with such a one. She's young and buxom. You won't have need of dreams, the dreams men need, not with that one.'

And so Sanchez had called at Emily's house and asked for her father, and asked her father for her, and been given the answer 'yes' because the name Sanchez was well respected and his great-great-grandfather was still remembered in the town.

And the 'yes' that he received had pleased Sanchez. And when in due time after receiving the 'yes' he received also Emily, he thought, in the first moment,

'Now I am a happy man.'

And it was true that in Emily he could find nothing to complain of. In his bed, she was compliant. When he guided her hand down onto his big testicles she did not draw it away. When he turned her over onto her stomach and fucked her hard from behind, she did not whimper. She did most of the things women did. She scrubbed the step and gossiped. She made him quite decent meals. Sometimes he stroked her stomach, which was smooth and velvety, and told her he loved her. It was then, perhaps, that he came nearest to complaining. For instead of smiling, as he would have liked her to smile, and saying,

'Ah Tiago, I love you too!' and making her lips curve into a full, tautened shape and showing the little ridged edges of her strong white teeth, instead of any of this, she would look at him, a strange, steady gaze, and rub her forefinger on the side of her nose, and put her hand up to the side of her head, and cover it almost as though she were in pain.

'What is it Emily?' he said to her now, turning his shoulder to the accusing eyes. 'Don't you feel well?'

'It is nothing, Tiago. Nothing,' she replied, pushing the counter-pane away from her and making as if to swing down her legs.

Sanchez was mesmerized by the sight of his wife's breasts as she half sat up. She had breasts such as belonged to none other. They were entirely separate breasts, extraordinary, at once so plastic and yet so very much alive. She saw him looking at her breasts and tossed her head and Sanchez looked away immediately and felt ashamed.

He supposed from the way she said nothing was troubling her that she was beset by women's things. He referred to all the strange goings-on of the female body as 'women's things'. These things were strange and incomprehensible. They made women seem to him infinite beings. If he thought about these women's things when he was in the physical act with his wife, then his desire would subside and the whole of him would shrink into impotence. A struggle went on within him now, between the desire his wife's breasts evoked and the strange sinking set in motion by her hint of the women's things. He said, without conviction,

'The boy will be late for school.' And then without waiting for her to reply, got up with an ungainly lunge, felt himself to be very ungainly as he stood on the mat quite naked, and conscious of the hair on his arms and back and shoulders, and conscious of how heavy his testicles were, lying on the inside of his thigh. He said,

'Never mind. If you're not well. Never mind, Emily. I'll see to the boy.'

Sanchez always referred to their one son as 'the boy'. He never referred to him by his given name. Perhaps he had forgotten what his given name was. His wife, too, seldom used it. Perhaps they had both forgotten.

Sanchez shook himself a little, as you might imagine a bear does, and got dressed quickly. Feeling the waistband of his trousers tighten around him was a relief.

When he'd gone out of the room his wife lay back again. The pillow was uncomfortable under her head and she adjusted it. She heard Sanchez call to the boy, and the sound of their footsteps as they went down the stairs together.

Later, quite a lot later, had Tiago Sanchez' wife been awake, she would have heard her husband and her one son bumping about in the small hallway, the boy picking up his hat and his bag of school books, the man putting on his blue working coat. Then she would have heard the door open and close, and the last metallic scratching as the latch dropped. But by the time these things happened, Emily Sanchez had gone back to sleep.

Tiago Sanchez walked along beside his son and thought,

'I am not a particularly happy man. I am not as happy a man as I thought I would be.'

He wondered if some fault in himself contributed to this lack of happiness. He had a wife who was faithful, a son, and a home he could call his own. These were the main constituents of what made a man happy. Of this he was convinced. And yet, he did not feel that complete feeling within himself that he took happiness to be. When he looked in the mirror, no happy man looked back at him. Sometimes he thought, I am rather a sad man, and the thought made him feel actively sad. The fact was, he should never have left La Braga. Leaving La Braga had been a big mistake. When he thought of how it had been in La Braga, the thought divided itself into two, there was the highly coloured, familiar image of La Braga, the texture and shape of which were so familiar he could feel them with the tips of his fingers, as though they had shape and substance quite outside his own imagination; and then there was the here and now, bitty and incomplete, grey and slated, with more or less symmetrical grey paved paths which reflected wetly the sepia skies of extended twilights.

'But will you like it, Tiago?' his father had said to him, sitting on the step and shredding tobacco in his fingers. 'Britain is not La Braga. To be Portuguese is different. To be any one thing as opposed to another, is more different than you would think.'

He had thought about what his father said to him. He wondered if he might discuss it with Emily, but saw her stirring the stew one night at the new white electric stove which was the envy of the other women, and thought better of it. Something in the way her shoulders were deterred him. He put aside the idea of going to England for three or four seasons. If you asked him, he could not have said whether it was three seasons or four, because a comparatively happy man does not measure time in seasons.

Emily had the boy. Some months went by in which he could not fuck her. This fuckless interlude gave him a chance to think. It is sometimes necessary for a man to reassess. He began thinking of England again. He thought about getting a job in a hotel. He had heard there were good openings in hotels. He mentioned what he had been thinking to his friend Bernardim one night when they were playing cards. The smoke from their cigarettes curled slowly upwards and wreathed itself around the electric light. Bernardim said,

'England! Ah, you always were a dreamer.'

And Tiago forgot about it in the excitement of losing heavily to his friend. And it fell away further from the conscious levels of his thinking when later that night he fucked his wife for the first time in some months. When he pressed up against her she didn't resist him, and he fucked her from behind and grasped both her breasts in his hands and felt them, as they had always been but somehow different, and smelled the milky smell of her in her skin and her fingers, where formerly what he had been most aware of was the mimosa scent she sprayed onto her neck and hair.

But the next day it was all round La Braga.

'That Tiago Sanchez,' the men said to one another, lifting their nostrils to the sharp tang of citrus which hung about their doorsteps and sank into the cool corners of their halls.

'He always bore the marks of an ambitious man. And who can

blame him? There's nothing in La Braga for a man of ambition.'

And the women looked enviously at Emily, it was something that one's husband was a little different, and one or two of them looked at Tiago differently and wondered how skilled he was, for all he was balding rather, in the act of love.

Nothing might have come of it. People forget things quickly. Tiago might just have said, as he did,

'Well. Nothing is decided,' and let the time go in thinking about it, because it is a fact that in thinking about things you can often get more pleasure than in the things themselves. But some few among us are cut out for greatness, or at least for the assault on greatness. And Tiago, perhaps, was one of these.

For some time, for more than a year on and off, he had been sitting for a head of Caesar. La Braga, despite its ordinariness, was not without distinction. For La Braga had a sculptor, a M. Woda, who had taken a house on the outskirts, coming without warning from the far side of the Pyrenees.

'But you have a head,' M. Woda said to Tiago Sanchez within the first minute. Tiago Sanchez thought this self-evident, but still it pleased him. And when M. Woda praised his profile, he began to think there was something in sculptors after all. M. Woda made etchings and did things in mezzotint. On the wall of his studio was an enormous drawing of a pregnant woman with her head thrown back and the veins in her breasts pencilled in ropy clusters. Tiago Sanchez agreed to sit for the head of Caesar.

'It's going to be noble,' M. Woda warned him. 'The head of Tiago Caesar will wear a laurel wreath!'

Although the whole thing progressed slowly, Tiago could see under the sculptor's hands a certain greatness come from nothing, from where there had previously been merely substance, order out of the chaos of the unmade.

'If M. Woda can make me into greatness, what can I not make of myself?'

This is the kind of thought that would be in Tiago Sanchez' head while M. Woda worked away, and there emerged from the tips of his fingers interlinked laurel and an unmistakable curvature of brow.

The head was almost ready by the time M. Woda got wind of Sanchez' plans.

'Don't say you're going,' said M. Woda, chipping away at a particularly difficult bit of chin. 'Not until I've finished this. Afterwards, well, that's a different matter. A man like you!'

And he gestured at the proud brow, and the angular cheekbones, and the way the hair curled up on one side to the lobe of the ear, a post-heroic gesture, the subtle execution of which pleased him.

Tiago Sanchez felt he couldn't express doubt. More than that, he felt doubt was unworthy of him. And there were things in La Braga which he chafed against. It was strange how the sun came up every morning always the same. It made the same shape on the wall next to the bed. And really, he should whitewash the bedroom. But he felt as though he didn't have the energy. His wife said to him,

'When are we going, Tiago? There will be preparations to make.' And he felt as if, without realizing it, he'd made up his mind.

He didn't like to think about how it was when he left La Braga. It made him feel ill in the middle. He felt as he had felt when he went to see his grandmother in the hospital and saw only her corpse. He felt restless and itched for his own doorstep. When a man stood on his own doorstep, things made sense. The first time he fucked his wife in England, the wallpaper by the bed had a pattern of blue roses. '*Blue!*' he said to himself. '*I ask you. What kind of a country have I come to?*' And the boy, in his cot next to the bed, made little whimpering noises as Tiago Sanchez ejaculated rather tardily into his wife.

He worked first in a hotel but fell out with the head chef, who said he wasn't the right type to work in a kitchen. And if the truth be told, he hadn't liked wearing an apron and a white paper hat which kept his curls away from his ears.

'The kitchen is really a place fit only for women,' he said to himself as he walked for the last time past the sign which said '*Hotel Entrance*', out into the swell of grey-coated people in the street, then onto the top deck of a red London bus which ferried him slowly west towards the single pink streak of a winter evening. He said the same thing to his wife when she put his dinner in front of him, and then brought in hers, and sat eating it quickly without looking at him, as if she were in a tremendous hurry, as if she had somewhere special to go.

Tiago Sanchez moved North with Emily and the boy. They found a terraced house on the edge of a small Northern town. When you stood in the Sanchez' triangular scrap of garden you could look out on the moor. Tiago Sanchez did this quite frequently, trying to make sense of it. He had bought the house on a mortgage. It was a very solid house. He had used up all his savings in it, but despite that, it was good to be able to say you owned your own house.

'There are plenty of people who don't own anything,' he said to Emily sometimes. He didn't always like the secret thoughts he believed he could see behind her eyes.

But he couldn't have said living in the North of England suited him. Actually, it got him down sometimes. He took a job in a factory which handled carpets and had a warehouse where they made up books of samples to go out to the shops. Sometimes you could have pieces of carpet free. Tiago took home as many as he could, and the Sanchez house was littered with them.

'Oh Tiago,' Emily would say to him. 'Why did you bring this bit? It's such an ugly colour. And it doesn't fit anywhere.'

But Tiago Sanchez knew you should have things when the chance presented itself. And you never knew when you'd be able to get just such a one again.

At the factory, the men called him San Tiago. Sometimes they made fun of him. He didn't like that. He thought about it after he had left the boy outside the school gates. It was really a bit early to leave him. But he was a good boy, quiet. And what else was there to do when

Emily got women's things? There were some things a man had to be thankful for. The boy was a good boy. But as he left his son he felt ill and uneasy. He wondered if he was sickening for something. He was a strong man but he'd had the influenza once or twice. The English climate didn't suit him. It was cold and damp.

The Foreman put him on stacking the shelves in the warehouse. When you were stacking shelves you spent the whole day going up and down a metal ladder with rolls of carpet on your shoulder. It was tiring because some of the rolls were heavy and big. Sometimes you nearly overbalanced. But Tiago was good at it, he had a natural monkey-like aptitude as he clambered about the racking and stacked the cylinders of carpet into neat symmetrical piles which grew and grew.

'Tiago'll show us. *San Tiago* knows the way!' the men joked. But by midday the sweat was standing out on Tiago's forehead in sculpted drops.

Word went around that Tiago wasn't well. Somebody got him an aspirin. He decided to lie down and rest instead of going in for his dinner.

It was not very easy to sleep on the narrow bed in the rest room, a high hard bed like the one you lie on in a doctor's surgery. But although it was not easy, Tiago slept. The room was rather stuffy and had one small window. It was very small, about the size Tiago's room was when he was a child. It reminded him, in a way, of that room. The walls were white. The floor had a small square rug at its centre.

When Tiago slept he dreamed he was back in La Braga. Perhaps that is not surprising. He dreamed he was a child again, and his grandmother had died. The death of his grandmother had a big effect on him. He sat on his own in his room and wept. The tears ran into the palms of his hands and made little lakes there. He rubbed at his eyes with the bunched knuckles of both hands. A fly came in through the small window and made a noisy reconnoitre of the room. Tiago imagined himself reflected in the facets of the fly's eyes, not one Tiago but several, like a set of photographic negatives placed side by side. The thought of the multiplication of himself cheered him momentarily. And then he thought of his grandmother, how she would never be reflected anywhere again, never be seen again, in single human vision or the fly's multiplied eyes. He sought vainly in his mind for a way of overcoming such obscurity. He wiped his eyes on his shirt tail and said,

'One day, I shall be famous.' It seemed to him then, if only his grandmother had been famous, he would not be losing her so totally. Of course, then he forgot about it. Life is not made for the famous. But he dreamt the whole thing again when he was asleep on the hard bed in the restroom with the aspirin lowering his fever a few degrees and the sweat draining into his navel and staining the underarms of his working shirt.

It felt very bad dreaming it again. He had actually just lost his grandmother. The real feelings were in the mind of the man as painfully and as powerfully as they had been in the boy. He thought,

'But this terrible feeling! I shall never get over it.' And twisted and turned on the bed as if he could physically get away.

When he woke up he felt bad and decided he would go home. It took him a while before he could believe he was not still in La Braga. One of the men said,

'Will you be alright, Tiago?' And another said,

'Come on! As if our *San Tiago* wouldn't know his own way home!'

When Sanchez got back to his house, no one was there. His wife had probably gone to fetch the boy from school. Something was cooking in the oven and the house was filled with a meaty smell. When he went into the bedroom the bed was very rumpled and smelled strongly of flesh. It came to him that he would not feel peaceful until he had seen his grandmother again.

'I must at least pay my respects,' was the thought that occupied him. 'I must lay a wreath at the base of the gravestone, under the date of her death.'

The thought made him feel more at ease. Nonetheless, he still felt ill, and slept intermittently until his wife came home.

Emily Sanchez nursed her husband with all the attention you could expect. It is usual for a wife to give attention to her husband under such circumstances. Tiago was ill for a month, and weak for another month after that. Tiago had never been weak before. His wife was surprised at how weak he could be. She said to him,

'Sit up Tiago, and I will make the pillows more comfortable,' and he sat up without any argument. And when she said to him,

'Come, Tiago, it is time for your pills now,' he raised his head and opened his mouth and put out his tongue like a little clockwork figure, not like her husband at all, who had fucked her too often for her liking, and of whom she had been secretly afraid. He seemed more humble, sitting in the kitchen with a rug over his knees.

Sometimes she forgot he was there, and hummed while she was making pastry. One night she came in with her coat on and said,

'Tiago, I'm going out for a while,' and one of the men from work was sitting with him, so he couldn't argue. The man diplomatically didn't mention anything, but Tiago was very tense for the rest of the evening and kept picking with his fingers at the edges of his red rug.

'My wife has been very good to me,' he said as the man left. But when she came in he complained and said things against her. But she just said,

'Don't be silly, Tiago,' and 'Isn't it time you were in bed?'

Although he felt rather weak he refused her help in getting upstairs. As he got ready for bed he was sweating. His hands shook as he folded his clothes. When he looked in the mirror he could see he was thinner. His chest was less deep than it had formerly been. He folded his clothes carefully and put them on a chair, and put on the jacket of his pyjamas but left the pyjama bottoms folded on the foot of the bed.

His wife was a long time seeing to the boy. He wondered if the boy could be ill, he seemed increasingly puny. It was difficult staying awake but he made a supreme effort and his eyes were still open when Emily tiptoed into the room.

Sanchez was not a patient man but he waited without saying anything to hurry his wife while she turned out the light and got undressed. It was strange to fuck her after two months. It seemed as if he were a different person, and she seemed different too. It was in the first few minutes afterwards, that strange empty space when the breathing is just getting back to normal, that he told her what he was intending about his grandmother's grave.

'If you say so, Tiago,' she replied, but her reply was muffled because she had her back to him, and it all sounded distorted, as if she were trying to stifle a yawn.

The visit to his grandmother's grave had been very much on Tiago Sanchez' mind during the two months of his illness. When his fever was very bad, he had hallucinations. He was there, kneeling on the paved surround, feeling the paving pressing deeply into his knees, and the smell of citrus tingling in his nostrils, and entering his nostrils and flowing deep into the inner recesses of his head. It was wonderful to feel a truly warm wind. He sat with his rosary wound around his fingers and felt extremely peaceful. The wreath he had placed on his grandmother's grave looked splendid. Everything was as it should be. And yet there was still a space that Tiago Sanchez wished something would fill. He had hoped his grandmother would in some way come to him. But the gravestone, with the date on it and the splendid wreath beneath, were stubbornly serene.

'I love you, granny,' he said, and the sky took it in and the wind whisked it away and the particular moment cradled it into a puff of nothing, and Tiago woke up with his wife's hand shaking his shoulder. But throughout his illness, Tiago's resolution to do the thing increased.

When he was well again he went back to work. The men were all pleased to see him and the Foreman let him take it easy for he first day. He hoped to work overtime almost immediately, because being ill is expensive and funds were low in the Sanchez household, and he needed to save up the money for his trip. But things had changed, there was no longer any overtime, people were being put on short days, the market for carpets was depressed. The men said it was the fault of the Government but Sanchez could understand, as far as he was concerned a carpet should last all your life. When he told his wife she said,

'Well, I don't suppose your grandmother is going anywhere.'

And for the first time in their married life Sanchez struck her cheek with the back of his hand. The boy, whom he hadn't noticed sitting in the corner, got up and went to his room. His wife cried bitterly and Sanchez apologised. But he was not really sorry. And he did not believe his wife was really hurt. The next day he went to the florist in his dinner break and placed an advance order for the most expensive wreath they made, and spent a very hungry afternoon piling up samples of carpet until his arms ached. When he got home, he found a letter from M. Woda and a photograph (long overdue) of the completed head. Tiago Sanchez searched the envelope in vain for the sum of money he hoped might be enclosed. When he found nothing he decided that perhaps there was, after all, nothing much to sculptors. And yet when he looked at the head he could not be other than proud of how it had turned out. It was noble. The line of the nose and the jawbone were very fine. M. Woda wrote that it was to be placed in a memorial garden at the back of the town hall in La Cidadela. Tiago Sanchez smiled. It was the nearest he had got for a long time to being a happy man.

A few weeks later he received a letter from the florist asking when he was going to call in his order. He went in personally and told them he still did not know. The assistant looked at him when he said it and he felt a fool. But since being ill he had been unable to make enough money to get the Sanchez family back on its feet. He told the assistant he would be calling in his order soon, maybe a few weeks, and she was to leave his requirements written in her order book.

At first he felt very uneasy at his failure to pay the respects he felt were due to his grandmother. He felt bad about it within himself, and when he saw himself in the mirror, shied away. Yet as the days passed, the thought became less of a sore thing. The boy was growing up and Sanchez took him fishing and it was pleasant to sit with him on the river bank and watch the flies rising in among the little wreaths of steam. It was summer and in the evening sometimes the river would steam and the steam would rise and then drop back onto itself as dew, and the small flies would rise and judder above the water until the low sun coloured them into nothing and then it got dark. Quite a few times Sanchez went into his bit of garden and looked at the moor which was extremely green at this season, and tried to make sense of it. His inability to do so bothered him less than it had done. He thought his son ought to learn cricket, and taught him first of all how to hold the ball. The seam of the ball felt real between his fingers. The curve of the ball felt heavy in the palm of his hand. His wife went out twice a week in the evenings. Occasionally he had letters from La Braga. His father and his mother were well. One of his sisters had made him an uncle again. The lemons – but did he remember the scent of the lemon groves? – the lemons were plentiful, thank God.

Sometimes late in the evening when the sun had gone down but it was still quite light, particularly to the North where the last of the light always seemed to settle, sometimes he would ask his wife to make a fire. The sight of the flames taking hold gave him pleasure. He would sometimes stretch out his hands and try to remember how warm it had been in La Braga.

'Is the fire alright for you, Tiago?' his wife would say to him, sitting back into her chair. His wife was putting on weight, she was more solid than she used to be, and she moved more ponderously. He fucked her much less frequently these days. She didn't seem to mind.

'Is the fire alright for you, Tiago?' she would say. And Tiago Sanchez would nod his fine head without replying and watch intently, like a man possessed, the first little curlings of smoke as they gathered over the coals and hung utterly still for a fraction of a second before beginning their slow spiral to the sky.

A Place in Wales

'It's out there. I know it is.'

The rhythmical squeak of the spinning wheel stuttered and slowed, the oscillating arc of its shadow on the farther wall came to a stop.

'You're imagining things,' said the woman, and cupped her two hands, one over each of her kneecaps, and eased the tension out of the back of her neck, and sat quite relaxed, her shoulders leaning slightly forward over her knees and her backbone curved so that you could see the diminishing knots of her vertebrae spoiling the smooth line of her shirt.

'You're tired, I expect. You've had a bad day. Why don't you go up to bed?'

The man waved away her suggestion and twisted irritably in his chair by the fire. He was a young man, younger than the woman, quite considerably younger. The firelight reflected on the flesh of his neck made him seem younger still, the skin so smooth and shiny, like a child's. He could almost have been her son, or perhaps a nephew, the single issue of some older sister.

He picked up the poker and dabbled the end of it into the red hot spaces between the coals. Although it was late April and the air outside was warm enough to be comfortable without a coat, he had insisted on a fire, on the grounds that the stone of which the old house was made gave off its own persistent chill.

The woman had acquiesced without saying anything, watching him get the twigs together and arrange them in the grate, watching him select little bits of coal, not so big that the twigs would burn out before the coal ignited, not so small they would be unable to form the core of the larger fire it was in his mind to build. There had been a moment, as there is with all fires, when she scarcely expected it to light, thought that the small flame sucking in air from underneath as it struggled up the side of the first twig would surely flicker and extinguish. But it had taken hold, and he had turned and smiled at her, there on his knees in front of the grate; a smile of triumph, a smile of satisfaction which forgot everything else, a smile contained in its own network of order, its own regularity of cause and effect, a child's smile which occurs so rarely in the faces of grown up men and women, and when it does is apt to blind those about them with its purity.

The woman had smiled back, adult and mechanical, a smile which stopped before it started, the brief shadow of it in her head reflected by the even briefer representation on her lips. Then she had left him to his fire and gone purposefully about the remainder of her day, making lists and ticking things off as she accomplished them, watching the hands of the clock revolve the hours around her, watching the light change shape, registering somewhere in her head how the mountains which surrounded the farmhouse grew denser as the sun slewed past the South and began its descent to the sea.

It was strange how, after rain, everything seemed very black. It had rained that morning, at about ten o'clock, a brief, hard shower which drummed on the roof and the earth and the backs of her hands as she reached for the latch of the casement window and pulled it to with a definite click.

'Why don't you leave it open?' he had said, coming into the kitchen with a plate with crumbs on it and an earthenware mug in which she could just see the dregs of one of his bitter, concocted drinks.

His special drinks irritated her. She thought, why did I have to marry a man who drinks green china tea? Then felt guilty about it almost at once because at least his drinks gave him something to think about, aromatic infusions whose presence filled the kitchen and seeped through the house, she could smell them clinging in the upstairs curtains, and scenting his breath when he came towards her.

She remembered his insistence on the fire and said nothing and left the window shut knowing that would be a statement in itself and doubting he would challenge it. She didn't really care. Her mind was already taken up with the blackening hills as the rain swept across them, grey bands of matter, specks of steel, great clumps of stuff deposited there at the blind end of the valley as though the opening of the clouds was part of some barely perceived but definite meta-physical intention.

She remembered the first time she had driven up the valley (it had been early October and the whole place was fiery with dying bracken) the thought had come to her, perhaps I shall find God here, which was a very strange thought because she had always, as far as she knew, been an atheist. But she had never thought it again and had not let it bother her, because that is the effect a radical change of place can have on you, it can do peculiar things to the usual balance of your mind, subvert the basis of the ideas you hold and always have held, knowing by logical deduction that they are right.

The next time she had driven up the valley was when they came for good. She didn't think about God this time, and the hills were particularly black. When you got out of the car the wind was enough to knock you over. Although it was only early afternoon, the light was already diminishing. She wondered why they had come.

But the next day the sun was out and the air was pleasantly crisp and the waterfall which you could hear constantly through the kitchen window made patient noises. Her husband had seemed enthusiastic. They made plans for Spring bulbs, and hens (six of them) and argued not very seriously about the merits of keeping a cockerel. Cockerels were so fine-looking. She imagined one strutting about the yard with his comb all red and glistening and his beak yellow and shiny and his 'cock a doodle do' so clear and pure it would reach the very tips of the hills and glance off them on its way out into space.

When she said this to her husband they both laughed. It was still in her head, them both laughing, and she took it out occasionally and looked at it, how their bodies swayed in towards each other and out again, with their heads thrown back and their eyes half closed, and the sound of it rising like colourless smoke. He had probably touched her. She thought she remembered the roughish feel of the hairs on the back of his hand. But she could not be sure.

In any case the cockerel had been decided against, it would make too much noise and possibly distract him, certainly would when he eventually got down to work. And the hens themselves, nothing had come of them, the hen house needed attention and neither of them knew what to do. Nor had they got around to planting the bulbs. She had bought a few, a dozen in a white paper bag one day when she went shopping, but they were still there, in the back of the kitchen drawer, sprouting no doubt, she didn't dare put her hand all the way in in case she touched them, shoots of things were so pale and fleshy, and the granular feel of them against her finger ends was sure to make her shudder.

Nor had her husband ever actually got down to work. The first week, they had set up a table in the small room at the far end of the bedroom, tucked under a corner of the eaves. They had laid in supplies of paper, and she had carefully put out a new pencil (in the only colour he would use, a deep, bright red) and a new silvery sharpener beside it, knowing how he said he could never write unless his pencil was sharp. At the end of November she added a paraffin heater and put up curtains to keep out the mid-winter wind. She thought perhaps he might find he wanted to write at night. She dusted his typewriter. But nothing had come of it. He occasionally went to the room and stayed there for an hour. She could hear him pacing, and once she caught him smuggling his radio up the stairs.

She told him not to be too disappointed, that it would take time to get back to things, to really recover. He didn't seem to listen, grew increasingly morose and spent hours walking up and down watching the waterfall carving its grey, curvilinear basin out of the stone. He became more reluctant to take his daily pills. He said,

'Pills! What have pills ever created but this vacuum in my head?'

She had to watch him closely to make sure he didn't just pretend to take them and hide them under his tongue and spit them surreptitiously into the sink. Once he said,

'It's living here. It's the silence. It won't let me think.'

But when they had driven back over the border, and the familiar

51

Englishness of things had closed over them, the fields and the hedges and the dirty grass verges spangled with fragments of black plastic bags, he had said he felt claustrophobic, and they spent a restless couple of days trying the patience of a long-suffering friend.

For a week he seemed glad to be back. He spent much more time shut up in the little room, and she actually thought he might be writing. It was at this time that she bought the spinning wheel, second hand, and a greasy fleece, and set up her own space in the corner of the big living room right at the far end away from the fire, just near enough to the window so that if she held her head at the correct angle, she could see out. He hadn't been pleased, and told her he thought it was a waste of time.

'Spinning,' he said. 'What's the point? Nowadays it's all done for you.'

But she said she found it relaxing, and time was something they both had plenty of. So she persevered and soon became quite expert, so that at first nearly every evening and then for quite significant parts of the day too you would find her seated at the spinning wheel and bowing her back to the rhythm of its steady revolution.

Her husband spent more and more time watching her. He seemed angry, but fascinated. It was as if he watched against his will. He was fascinated by the way she drew out the yarn, how the yarn drew out and out until there was miles of it hanging in skeins about the place like ropy cobwebs. The smell of it went up his nose and into the centre of his head until he became convinced the last thing on earth he would be aware of, at that one culminating moment when the soul leaves the body and the human relic casts itself into the nerveless abysses of eternity, the very last thing would be the smell of freshly spun wool, and the rapid twist of his wife's white fingers, blind and hideless as baby snakes.

He didn't bother to go up to the little room now. The papers on the desk grew damp and bent up at the edges and dust settled into the curves the bent up edges made. She didn't like going into that room any more. It had that emptiness about it you get when someone has died. Absence, intensified by a strong sense of former presence. Mould began to grow over the deep wall by the window. There were rustlings in the rafters above and she guessed something was nesting.

Her husband began to have bad nights. He said he didn't like the moon rising into the roof light and filling it entirely, so she cut up a makeshift curtain which she drew just before getting into bed, but as he slept better she slept badly, suffering from claustrophobia because she could no longer see the stars.

Their long-suffering friend came and enthused over everything and said,

'God, you're so lucky to have a place like this, a place in Wales where you can get away from everything.'

He paced the width of the sitting room and said how spacious it was and knocked his head on the beam which ran across the centre, and set the spinning wheel turning with the top of his finger and said, 'Ah! The good life! There's nothing like it' and slept well despite the silence which he didn't like to admit even to himself he found rather frightening.

'Got a few potholes!' was the last thing they heard him say as he bumped off down the drive, trailing his hand out of the window like a tattered flag.

Dear Bernard she thought, very glad he hadn't stayed.

'He's a pain in the arse,' her husband said, and slouched off to his vigil by the waterfall.

Her spinning soon took over. The little scullery at the back of the house was festooned with yarn dyeing and drying, great hanks of it, brown and yellow and green and pink and purple. You could hardly move in there because of it. He told her the spinning thing was getting out of hand, but instead of being sorry, which a man might expect when his wife knows something she does affects him, she threw back her head and let out a peal of laughter. She was getting very jolly nowadays. He didn't like the way her neck arched when she threw back her head and he could see the smooth weals of tissue which made up the texture of her throat.

One day he caught her talking to a rough-looking man with two sheep dogs writhing at his heels. She was leaning over the gate talking to the man seemingly quite at ease despite the fact that the gate was wet and the rust was rubbing itself in big brown patches onto the clean fronts of her clothes. He hadn't got time for neighbours. Neighbours were one of the things he had wanted to get away from. He didn't go up to them but hovered in the background waving a bit of stick aimlessly and listening to the distant guttural sounds coming out of the man, he looked very rough and his hair was hanging down behind his ears, poking out under his cap in a grey frill. The man laughed once or twice, a short, whinnying sound. The woman looked over her shoulder but other than that gave no sign that she had noticed her husband. Later she said,

'That was our neighbour. Why didn't you come up?'

And getting no answer other than a grunt went on,

'He said his name's *Hedd*. I think it means "peace".'

And still getting nothing from him, settled herself at her spinning wheel and began deftly to draw out the thread.

She no longer thought very much about whether her husband was working. His unhappy face, with the lines of it all drawn downwards and his earlobes seeming almost to touch his shoulders, so much did he nowadays sink into himself, she saw as if entirely from outside, as though they were the dreary accoutrements of a stranger. She felt sorry for him, and attended his needs quite assiduously, much as if she had been his nurse. She didn't like the way he watched her. It put her on edge. What she liked best was drawing out the thread, and planning in her head the patterns she would weave it into. First of all there would be a rug with triangles of red and blue, just a small rug, something quite small to begin with, because she had never woven anything before. Then a bigger rug, perhaps full room size, well, for a small room anyway, creams and greens alternately, with unexpected jagged bits of saffron. And then there would be.... But the possibilities were almost endless, the permutations of colour and pattern dazzling in their variety. In fact the first thing she made, because she had not yet got a loom, was a carefully crocheted belt. She had so much wanted to make something out of her beautiful skeins of wool, she couldn't wait for the loom, which she had chosen from a catalogue and ordered. So she crocheted a long belt (far too long, it would have gone round her own quite thin middle at least twice), using up all her colours and done in a tight mosaic pattern reminiscent of the headband she thought might have adorned the forehead of some ancient Inca deity. The result pleased her. She liked the way the colours fused when you looked at them quickly, as though a harmony had been achieved by her own chosen juxtapositions which was beyond anything she had hoped for. Her husband didn't like the very tight pattern. He said,

'My psychiatrist would have a ball with that one.'

But she refused to trouble herself with repression and envy and angst and dislocation, and delighted in the bright geometry her own hands had created.

She put a hook in the wall next to her spinning wheel and hung the belt there and admired it, sometimes consciously, sometimes in the back of her mind where it swayed as the winds of her imagination caught it up, like an enticing, multi-coloured flame.

The night by the fire, after the rain, when her husband had his very bad feeling (he was getting them frequently now, afraid of whatever lay outside the boundaries of himself, afraid too of what was within) she suggested he should go up to bed. He went, pressing his weight onto each of the wooden stair-treads so the whole thing seemed to shudder and she thought, 'Those stairs! Something will have to be done!'

That night, after she had finished her spinning, at about eleven o'clock or perhaps it was half past, she sat quietly doing nothing for a few minutes and enjoying the bright belt hanging on its makeshift hook. She touched it once or twice and it felt good against her fingers. She thought, perhaps before the loom came she would make another. She liked making things. It quite surprised her.

When she had raked out the last of the fire and turned out the light, she went to bolt the back door, but opened it instead and stepped outside. It was very still. Even the waterfall seemed unusually subdued, and the smell of fresh things, some late buds and a flurry of young grass, sharpened up her nostrils and she lifted her head a little, like a dog sensing something coming from a long way off. It was also very dark indeed, a blackness filling the valley to the rim, and above the rim the sky invisible, not even the punctuation of a star.

She went in and shut the door and went upstairs with an uneasy feeling, but felt calmer when she saw her husband sleeping with his hand clenched against the side of his face, as a child sleeps.

She took off her clothes and folded them and got into bed with nothing on and lay against her husband's back and fell asleep herself quite soon. In the night he was very restless, much more restless than he had ever been. His restlessness woke her up, and it must have been five before she eventually went back to sleep, but even then uneasily, as if she was half aware that at any moment some random movement of her husband might disturb her again.

She didn't wake up until quite late, gone eight o'clock, feeling anxious, with that guilt and fear you tend to get when you are late, even though you may have nothing particular to do. Her husband was already up, which was unusual, a dent in the pillow where his head had been, and the sheets thrown back as though he had got out in a hurry. She lay on her back and listened, expecting to hear him moving about somewhere in the house. But it was quite quiet. The sun was just coming up over Craig y Ffynnon, the clear square of the roof-light etching itself onto the farther wall.

She got out of bed hastily and pulled on some clothes. She didn't stop to do up her sandals, and they made a brash, slapping sound as she ran down the stairs.

'Ted!' she called. 'Ted?' And thought, where can he have got to?

She went into the sitting room and the first thing she saw was that her belt had gone. The empty hook looked startlingly solid, casting a short, blunt shadow on the wall. The woman swayed slightly, as you do when you begin to feel faint, everything recedes and you balance for that instant on the pinhead of existence. She thought, I ought to keep calm, and put her hand onto her ribs as though she could control her heart beat by exerting pressure there.

She did up her sandals and walked quickly out into the yard and listened and then went across to the barn and pushed open the tall doors which swung apart with a creak. The interior was cavernous and placid. The great, dark rafters, punctuated by spots of light where the roof was going, were undisturbed. She said,

'God. *God.*'

Outside again she blinked and headed for the waterfall. Even before she got there she saw, or thought she saw, a flash of it, and a step or two later she *did* see it, her own precious belt, harmlessly adorning her husband's highish forehead as he sat on a rock by the stream with his dark red pencil in his hand and an exercise book poised industriously on his knee.

She said his name and he turned irritably towards her, but then smiled, a preoccupied kind of smile, and turned back to his work. Later, back in the house and ticking things off on a list as she accomplished them, the woman's desire to strike her husband, the momentary overwhelming wish to see him dead, had almost entirely abated. She listened with tolerable composure as he went up the stairs, and when she heard the hard, twofinger rhythms of his typewriter begin, was nearly indifferent.

She didn't sit down to her spinning because the noise of the treadle and the wheel constantly turning was sure to disturb him. Towards the end of the afternoon she saw him going past the window with his hands in his pockets and his head held back, at an angle, he looked as if he was whistling.

Later, much later, she went up to the bedroom and through into the little room tucked under the eaves and saw her belt hanging on the back of his chair. She picked it up and folded it in two and replaced it carefully. Then she tidied together the four typed sheets her husband had left spread out on his table and placed on top of them a fifth, blank but for the title typed in capitals, *A PLACE IN WALES*, and an inch or two below it, also in capitals, his name.

CHARITY

At the wedding she had said 'Yes', and 'Until death'. That was a long time ago and her hair was quite grey now, and her eyes were marooned in a sea of little wrinkles.

Alessandro saw them, the eyes and the wrinkles, when he knocked at her door. She was a typical, timid woman who answered his knock, too many years without a man, too many days and nights in the long bed (bought to accommodate her husband, surely, because she was a very short woman) alone.

Alessandro held out the collecting box, and seeing the refusal begin to form in her, the tensing of the muscles in her neck and the start of the side to side movement of her head that would send him back down the steps empty handed, he said,

'It's a good cause.'

What he really said was, 'Ees a good cau-sa,' because he found English difficult, having only recently, and reluctantly, given up a longstanding career at sea.

'I deen wanna,' he said to his one friend Elis, who was also an exile, having settled by accident in the county after spending most of his life in the North.

'I deen wanna.'

But what else, his accompanying shrug seemed to indicate, can a man do?

'Ees a good cau-sa,' he repeated, standing on her top step with the wind that funnelled up the street, and before that, up the valley that became the street, lifting the blunt ends of his straightish hair.

He shook the collecting box and the coins inside rattled. The wind brought with it the smell of living in a strange place. He knew many of the smells of the different places in the world. Rio, Santiago, Durban, Quatar. Now he smelled the particular smell of this small part of a small country. It had nothing to do with politics. The smell of a place was made up of its weather and its history. That was how he wanted to think of it. It wasn't as simple as that but he wished it to be simple, because he had led a complicated life and it had tired him, and now he wanted to lead a simple life, and feel the tiredness leave him, and sense himself to be at peace.

He shook the box again and said,

'Anything....'

She moved her head from side to side, very firmly this time, with just the right balance of decision and condescension, lengthening her neck a little so that the large lapels of her flowered blouse could assert themselves.

'No,' she said, in a soft voice that was definite too. He thought that she had probably been a schoolteacher. Either that, or a District Nurse. He could imagine her quelling unruly children with a look. He could imagine her too in uniform, closing her front door at dawn or before dawn, pulling it to behind her with a click and getting into her dark little car and feeling the hem of her gabardine raincoat rasping her stockings as she adjusted her legs.

He was going to say something more to try to persuade her but she had already closed the door, almost, and the only thing that was left of her was an eye. And what an eye it was, he said to himself afterwards, walking along with the collecting box hanging by its two strings from his wrist. It was an eye that was ageless and placeless. It was Eve's eye. It was the eye of every woman he had made love to, and of most of those he had fucked.

Alessandro (it was a nickname, he had been baptized Guiseppi) was widely experienced in women. He had fucked women in most of the countries of the world. He had made love to women rather more selectively, perhaps in only two or three countries. There had been a few boys too, Morocco had been bad that way, for temptation, but he did his best to forget about those experiences. There were things it was better not to let in, they cluttered up your life, they made it difficult for you to be at peace.

That evening, when he was sitting on the bench by the war memorial waiting for Elis (it was a warm enough June, and girls with their legs all bare and little cotton tops that their breasts pushed out of were walking up and down) he thought of the woman again. She was fifty, or more than fifty. He thought of her body and knew what it would be like, because he had measured the decay of his own. He had measured the decay and hated it. His own age, other people's age; he hated the fact that youth was naturally fuckable and age was not. If he had been a different kind of man he would have taken to drink. As it was he confined himself to moderation and maintained a certain terseness in his dealings with his inner and regretful self.

When Elis came he asked him who the woman was, knowing already, because he had asked at the shop, that she was Miss Thomas, Gwynfryn. She was a relative newcomer and kept very much to herself.

'They say she came from Pontypridd,' Elis said. 'But then, I've heard too, that she came from Abergavenny.'

Elis said it rather mournfully. He was a mournful man, recently widowed. There was loneliness in the angle of his cap. They sat on the bench talking quietly and irregularly for half an hour or an hour, watching but not watching the girls walking up and down and the boys, who sat on the wall together and swung their legs, and pushed their hair back off their foreheads and then, after a suitable interval, let it fall forwards again.

The only thing left of her was an eye. It was the eye that he remembered throughout the following day, as he went from house to house with his legs getting heavier and his heart feeling large under his ribs.

'A good cau-sa,' he said, again and again. And most of the men and women agreed.

At the end of the afternoon he climbed the steps to the Town Hall and went in past the Corinthian pillars (too grand entirely for the building, and the building itself too grand for the town, but that was how they had done things in the old days, you could see it in all the big old buildings, the sense of getting ahead of yourself, the idea of somewhere big and important where, with a little effort, anyone could go).

He offered his collection box to be counted, and sat down to wait. The room, which was a large room with high ceilings and a cornice, contained, as well as the tables where people were counting out the money, displays of all the uses the place had been put to over the years. There were photographs of it turned into a hospital during the war. Then in the first war, as a recruitment office. Alessandro recognized a picture of Kitchener. Then there was a faint, yellowy-looking photograph, the steps packed with people and a banner with Welsh words on it that he couldn't understand, and a banner with English words that he could.

'That,' Elis said when he asked him about it later, 'was the investiture of the Prince of Wales. Nineteen hundred and two, I think it was. Anyway. A long time ago.'

Then there was tea, at the Coronation. A party for the Silver Jubilee. Brass band competitions. The crowning of Miss Miskin, a plain little girl with hair straggling on her shoulders. A rally, during the miners' strike. Boxing contests, and wrestling, on a Saturday afternoon.

The wrestling held Alessandro's interest. The other pictures had bored him. It was not, after all, his country, and all the pictures seemed to be of grey, indistinguishable faces. But the last picture of all was of two women wrestling, and it held his attention because it reminded him that once two prostitutes had pretended to fight over him. He had forgotten, because it was a long time ago, exactly where. Perhaps it had been one of the Mediterranean ports, but he thought not. It had more the feel of South America to it. Anyway, they had pretended to fight over him, and his shipmates had been envious. He couldn't remember which of the women had won. One had been darker than the other. One had been very thin. Had the dark one been thin? Or had the thin one had lighter hair, almost a reddish kind of colour, which grew down onto her forehead in a peak? It was odd how you remembered sometimes, the littlest of things. Afterwards he'd had both of them, the first in a proud way, offering his body as a kind of prize. The second he'd treated more gently, feeling for an instant an unfamiliar desire to console.

He hadn't thought about it from that day to this. But he thought about it now, and it made him restless, and he leaned forward and looked at the photograph closely, the one woman, fleshy and blonde-looking and with a lot of black stuff around her eyes, the other, darker and more wiry altogether, with her hair cut off short around her face, and a defiant look as she stared at the camera, the corners of her mouth pulled in tight. 'Mad Marge' the caption under the photograph said. 'Mad Marge v Jinny the Giantess. September 1963.'

*

And when I said 'Yes', Marged said (going to the window and looking out to where the grass was growing on the landscaped part, very green indeed all the way up the hill, but too smooth to be a real hill, and with a few black bits showing however much they tried to hide them, in between).

When I said 'Yes', I hadn't meant yes in the way people mean it, the forever kind of yes that lives with you and becomes part of you and you can't get away from. I meant the *for now* yes, this minute, today, this week. But Yeses had a habit of catching you. Noes were safer. And all that time ago she'd said Yes, just for the sake of it, really.

'Marged,' he'd said looking very sorry for himself one night, sitting in her Mam's back kitchen on the way home from the pub. And she'd said, almost without meaning to, it was strange when she heard herself say it,

'Very well, Ifor.'

It was a grown-up thing to say.

And after they were married, he stood at the foot of the bed and took his clothes off, one by one, his tie, his shirt, his socks, his underpants (she had looked the other way when he unbuckled his belt). He had stood at the foot of the bed, at last with nothing on at all, and his body rather thin and drab, and a thin streak of shadow under the curve of every rib, and almost directly under the electric light, so that his body looked elongated a little, although it cast no shadow, which was strange because everything else in the room had a rather black shadow attached to it. When she had seen him like that, she knew the true nature of the mistake she had made, and knew also that it was not something she could put right, not ever, because now she had done it it was part of what she was, and your self was one thing you couldn't get away from, no matter how long, or how earnestly, you tried.

In the event, it was Ifor who had got away from her. Not that even that was true, really. He had never been hers, although he might have liked to be. And she had certainly never been his, except in the exchange of her body for his name, and in doing the things a wife does, like a maid really. Her mother had been a maid before the war, up at Canal Head House. Marged had seen a photograph of her with her hands clasped in front of a little white spoon-shaped apron, and another little bit of something white, with primped-up edges and a visible kirby-grip, settled precariously in her hair.

'Ifor not back for the weekend?' her next-door neighbour Eirianfa said. (Eirianfa came from Dolgellau originally, and went back there not long after, the South never really suited her, it was impossible to settle, somehow, in the strange, pale air.)

'Ifor not back?'

Marged had said to herself, when she was a child, that she would never be anybody's maid. There was an old snapshot, quite bent around the edges, of her in a sunbonnet, staring out fiercely from the deep shade the brim cast across her face. She was waving a stick at the camera, and the little cluster of lumps that was her knuckles stood out.

'Fierce, by God,' Ifor had said when she showed it to him, the only time, really, she had showed him anything. The way he said 'Fierce' troubled her. He said it with that look she didn't like in men, the mouth too relaxed, and the pupils of his eyes taking on a dark look, and the muscles in the neck tightening and then going slack again.

When Ifor had left, eventually, not letting her know beforehand, just not coming back, and getting a friend to write her a letter, an English friend, they were working on the new road near Ross (the letter had a Hereford postmark), when Ifor had left she felt strange, and separate, and missed for a few nights the idea of him taking his socks off at the bottom of the bed.

'Ifor not back, then?'

Ifor will never be back. Ifor will never lift the latch on the gate, and take the three steps you have to take to get to the door, and open it, and come in, bringing with him the smell of the outside, the town in his coat and in his hair, the smell of exhaust fumes, the cold wind under his fingernails.

Behind the house where she had a room, in Cardiff, in a small street that didn't lead anywhere, was a dug-up piece of earth, with primroses on one side, and daffodils on the other, and the brown-coloured bits of what was left of the snowdrops in between. (My life has been made up of back yards, and half-turned earth. And the walls of the houses going up very straight, and the roofs, in layers, angling back over themselves.) There was a lot of traffic and the shop windows were very shiny and you saw, as you went past them, your own reflection coming at you from different angles. It didn't seem like you. You were no longer the person you had thought you were, but another person who looked rather like you but wasn't. (And what is this strange sense every morning, waking up, of my self getting smaller and smaller, like an island in the middle of a river rising in flood?)

'You,' the man said, and pointed at her, there, in a line, waiting to see if you were any good at it, looking at you first as you walked up and down in a swimming costume, looking at you very closely indeed as you waited, your tum three away, then next-but-one, then next, and the others already there and doing it, or having done it, the grunting and the falling, the pretending, and the odd occasional blow that caught you like a fiery and exploding thing.

The man's forefinger was stiff and straight at the end of his straight arm.

'You!' The finger moved twice, from the joint.

She stepped forward. She felt like a schoolgirl. She felt as she had done sometimes in Chapel, on a Sunday. If there had been any excuse for it, that would have been different. If she had done it for any of the reasons women do things, any of the old reasons –

'You!' the man said.

And then she stopped thinking about it and climbed up, with big, fluid movements, into the ring.

Now, Marged. What was it like? (looking out over the landscaped part and counting the black bits, one, two, three, four, see how they all link up and make a pattern, like veins the black bits are, snaking in and out of the green).

When she had first come there, nearly thirty years before, everything had been black still. The wheel had been turning, the spokes of it all in a blur. Strange how memory took away the colour. The sky had been white. She had climbed up into the ring and felt the top rope scrape at the skin of her shoulder, and the middle rope press into the flesh of her thigh and then spring loose again as she let it go. She had stood up in that square free space that took away entirely and for the allotted time her freedom, and felt cut off from everything that she knew and was, from everything that she had ever dreamed of, or wanted to be. And yet, how solid the sweat had felt running down her back, and down her ribs at the sides under her arms. How real the faces were still, and the room, hot and tight on her, and the air thick with the tail ends of words. She never knew for certain whether she had been more herself at those times, or less.

'Stick to what you know,' her mother had urged her once, fiercely, although her voice was getting very thin. But sometimes knowing (she had come to understand) can be more of a burden than a relief.

And what do I truly know? (staring in the mirror in the room in Cardiff, with her back to the window, and the patch of earth unturned now behind her, and treacly-looking in the uncentred light).

What do I truly know?

There had been a man she went to bed with sometimes, but intermittently. His body had been solid and his steps definite on the linoleum as he collected up his clothes. And something in it had brought her afterwards back to this half-known place, rather like Eden, the old pictures of it, sketches in Borrow, *Wild Wales*. Eden no longer. (She had heard her mother speak of the boy from Canal Head House riding his pony up on Ferndale, late in the afternoon).

And yet it was in a way like Eden. Quiet, her house. Peaceful before the fall. The clock ticked. The flames in her gas fire made little whiffling noises when the wind backed round. She had pointed herself, like a weather vane, in this inevitable direction. She did not long for, she resented rather, the sound of a step on her step, the rasp of the knocker, tentatively yet deliberately raised.

Who is it? she called, in her head perhaps, because it was evening now and the children who played outside in the street had gone in, and a certain thickening in the outline of things told you it would soon be dark.

Who is it.

*

Alessandro took his hands out of his pockets. The edge of his pockets rasped over his knuckles as he withdrew his hands. A cool current of air wound up the street towards him and threaded itself between his ankles and slid up over his shoulders and around his neck. He put his head on one side at an awkward angle and looked up past the dark shape of the hill rising away. The sky was a colour he had never seen before. It was the colour he thought it would be the first time he crossed the equator. A dark, indescribable colour. He settled his weight back on his heels. Something ticked inside him, like a metronome. The street, where it fell away quite steeply, was dull under the lack of stars. A light came on inside the house, and went out again. He felt the wind lodge in a series of cold little bars under his fingernails. The town was yellow now below him, the hill black and solid-looking behind. He wondered whether he should knock again. He strained for a sound of something inside the house, but there was only the wind out there with him, and the curious half darkness lapping the promontories of his hands.

THE CHOCOLATE FACTORY

The day the letter from the chocolate factory came, Micah had over-slept and was still in bed. She hadn't really overslept. But she lay with her eyes closed and her mind wholly disengaged, pretending to herself that she was still asleep, and couldn't hear the commotion as the postman pushed the letter through the metal flap, and the dog raced into the small hallway barking and generally making a hulla-baloo, and her mother followed the dog, slowly because her bad hip was playing up, and picked the letter up off the coconut mat (which was badly in need of replacing, it was getting very frayed) and turned it over slowly in her stiff fingers, and squinted down at it, trying to make out who it was to.

Although Micah wasn't really asleep, she wasn't wholly awake either. She was in her favourite limbo state, where anything was poss-ible, she could be anyone and go anywhere and take herself off on the strong stuff of her imagination, out of the small bedroom at the back of the house, out of the house itself with its relatively tidy grassed back yard, out of Perry Common (that was a laugh – it could-n't have been a Common for about a hundred years and the only grass you could see was littered with dogshit and condoms and the crumpled plastic bags the kids dropped when they were sniffing glue) – out of the city even, and away to places she had read about, down South where people lived in big houses with landscaped gardens and garages for three cars, or abroad, to places she had seen pictures of in the colour magazines she looked through when she went to the dentist, places with bright green trees, deep blue sea (she had been to Clacton once when she was little, and the sea hadn't been a bit the same), and pale yellow beaches with no one on them, except just her, a bit older so she had more of a bust, and tanned, tanned all over like the models were, or Miss World, and lying back on a flowered lounger, with a handsome looking man pouring something sparkling into a long glass.

It was wonderful to dream. But dreaming didn't get you anywhere, at least, that was what her mother said. She wondered sometimes where there was to get to, if not the pale yellow beaches fringed by green trees, which she felt sure she would never actually get to, particularly now she had failed her exams.

'Qualifications is what counts,' her mother had said, back in the Spring when she should have been revising, but instead spent nearly every evening sitting upstairs in her room with the books unread in front of her, staring out of the window at the skyline of roofs and towers and concrete chimneys which lit up as the sun went down, and haunted her strangely. What was it about the skyline and the way it changed? It was almost as if something else was behind it, there was what you saw, and then something under what you saw, something else which she felt but couldn't identify, which made her feel restless and strange. Sometimes she felt like that when she looked at pictures. Not all pictures, just some. Pictures of people's faces. A print of some yellow flowers in a vase that was hung up in the hall at school. Those flowers! They looked like they were alive! She had often watched them out of the corner of her eye, standing about waiting to go into Assembly, watched them in a half fearful kind of way, almost afraid they would leap out of their frames and take on some new and active life. They never had, of course. But it didn't stop her believing in the existence of something-under-the-surface. She never said anything about it. Her mother had enough to worry her and her friend Imelda (she hadn't seen her since the day they left) would never have understood.

But something under the surface, her own particular insight, her double vision of the world, hadn't helped her when it came to the Summer term, and the claustrophobic classroom with its forty bent heads and the rustle of turned over pages and the faint friction of ideas being shaped onto paper, and the halffuttered communal sigh as the sections of time measured themselves off on the circular clock at the far end of the room. After three weeks of suspense she found, with only a little surprise, that she had failed everything.

Her mother said,

'But Micah, you were such a clever little girl! Y' talked way before any of my friend's kids. Y' did great in the Junior school. What has happened to you, child? What has happened along the way?'

Micah had stood sullenly in the kitchen and watched the veins throbbing in her mother's swollen ankles, how very brown her flesh looked above the pale pink fluff decorating the edge of her bedroom slippers. Micah was much paler, with a pale gold skin which had caused a white boy at school to sit in the desk behind and whisper '*half caste bastard!*' at the back of her neck, so quietly only she could hear, all the way through a Social Studies lesson on racial equality. When she got home that day she went straight into her bedroom and picked up the mirror and took it to the window where the light was better and stared at herself for a long time, probably an hour or more, until she heard her mother letting herself into the hall, and her uneven movements as she limped through into the kitchen, and the sound of the fridge door opening, and the chink of milk bottles being put on the shelf.

It wasn't fair! She had said as much once, tentatively, to her friend Imelda, who had stared at her hard and then laughed and said,

'Oh, grow up!' and offered her a cigarette.

'You wanna forget all this pathetic stuff,' her friend Imelda had said. 'Y'know, about getting on, and that. Have a good time! That's what I say. You should try it.'

And she had winked and lost interest and waved and giggled at a gang of workmen who were lounging on a bench just outside the school gate, one of them had his blue overalls open to the waist, and the muscles of his neck were tight and shiny in the sun. Micah watched how her friend Imelda went over to speak to them. She looked different, older somehow. She walked differently, and held her head at an angle. One of the men gave her a cigarette, and Micah saw her accept it with a queer kind of duck and bob, like a movement they had learned in some old fashioned dance once, when the weather was bad and they'd had to do PE inside.

Micah didn't much like men. They smelled peculiar and had big hands and fingers. She felt instinctively it was better for women to live together. As far as she knew, she had no memory of the time her father had lived with them, a seldom mentioned white man who left just after she was born.

'That bas-tard!' was all her mother had said. Micah was fascinated by the careful way her mother accentuated it, short 'a', then a very definite 'r' before the 'd', which produced little bits of froth which hung on the perimeter of her lips. Certainly it was better to live with women. And yet, there were women who earned her mother's scorn, there was a woman who called herself Mrs Tyler and lived three doors down, now *there* was a woman her mother wouldn't even pass the time of day with.

'That stinking whore,' was how her mother referred to her, and passed her without recognition on the other side of the street (though Micah had seen once or twice how her mother had watched Mrs Tyler out of the corner of her eye, when she thought no one was looking).

Mrs Tyler apart (who wore a lot of make up and went out at night in a white fur jacket and black high heeled shoes), Micah preferred women. She wished it had been a woman who interviewed her the first time she went about a job, but it was a man, a middle-aged man in a tweed jacket with a red tie which accentuated the redness of his forehead and cheeks.

'I didn't like him much,' she said to her mother.

'What d'he say about a job?' her mother said to her.

He hadn't said very much about a job. Only,

'What? No exams at all?'

And when she had said,

'Well. P'raps I could move, y'know, go and work on a farm or something,' he hadn't even bothered to answer, just looked through her, so she had immediately felt very small, much as she had done on her first day at school (she remembered it clearly, though it was such a long time ago) when the fear and the excitement had all but overcome her, and she had peed down her left leg and into her shoe. She still remembered the shame and the heat of it, all intermingled, and with it the brief good feeling of relief, but then all too soon the clammy, unclean feeling, and the hoots of laughter, and the shame.

The man had taken down a few notes about her, but he hadn't seemed very interested, and she was conscious all the time of all the others waiting in the plastic chairs outside, school leavers like her, quite a lot of them white, and the man was aware of them too, and kept looking past her and through the glass door.

'He didn't say much' she said to her mother. 'Expect I'll go on the dole.'

Her mother didn't answer but her face crumpled up. It wasn't that she cried. You couldn't even say that her eyes got that veiny, wet look people's eyes get when they are going to cry. It was just that all the lines in her face seemed multiplied a hundred fold, the creases split into crevasses, so deep you couldn't tell where they ended, or if they ever did.

'He said I might get something. Just, y'know, to wait.'

She had said that to comfort her mother, without really believing it. And as the weeks went by, the idea of getting something faded from both their minds. And it was pleasant for Micah's mother to have her there.

'The tea always ready on the table when I get in,' she said to her friends with an appropriate accent of pride.

Micah didn't know how it had happened, but her mother treated her differently, she was more like a much older friend than her mother, and hardly ever criticized. And it was nice as the Winter came on to draw the curtains in the kitchen against the descending darkness and the fizzy yellow street lights, and sit at the table with the gas rings left on and enjoy talking to her mother about how things used to be, the way it was when her mother first came over, all sorts of things, except the only thing they never talked about (which was nice, too, in a way) was men.

And there was more time in the day when the house was empty, for Micah to settle back into her imagination. In her mind she could be anyone. In a way it was better to be what you wanted to be just in your head. In your head, you never met with difficulties, your existence was effortless. She found it hard sometimes to come back. One day her mother said,

'You alright, Micah?'

And when, with an effort she had brought herself back to the kitchen and the sink and the tea and her mother's wet coat hanging on the back of the door, her mother stared at her and said,

'You seem kinda strange to me.'

But usually she left herself enough time and was only a little impatient for the evening to pass and the night, until she could see her mother off in the morning and look forward to another beautifully vacant day. The vacant day was like a huge blank sheet of paper on which her mind drew things. Although, when she thought of it, that wasn't quite true, the things seemed to create themselves, to form themselves out of the blankness into scenes and people, places and times and movement and speech and laughter. It all formed itself down to the last detail. The chink of a cup and saucer, the strange grating sound a teaspoon made stirring the sugar in the bottom of the cup. Sometimes the way it was, how everything meshed in together, hurt her, she just wanted to shield herself from the denseness of it. At other times she wanted to retain what she had made. She didn't like the way it faded out of her head and became nothing, when each imagined day faded out of her head she felt bereft.

'Maybe I could do something,' she thought.

The only bad thing in this time was the signing on. The concrete building you went into was ugly looking. She didn't like standing in the queue. It made her ashamed. She got out as quickly as she could, and caught the first bus home, and felt better as soon as the familiar chimneys of her own street came into view, and better still when the bus pulled up and she got off and walked along the well-known pavement to her own front door.

'It's nice to be home,' she sometimes said to her mother.

'No place like home,' her mother said, and smiled at her, and turned up the television.

The letter from the chocolate factory came in late November and was an unpleasant surprise. The first thing her mother said was,

'What about the dog?'

They had got a dog from the RSPCA the month before. Micah liked the dog and took it out occasionally, when it wasn't raining, for a walk.

'You can't come home in the middle of the day. Not from the factory. Who's going t' let the dog out?'

Micah said maybe she wouldn't get the job, it was only an interview. But they both knew better. And after a single interview the chocolate factory took Micah on, and she became M SIMMONS FN 8621, and they gave her a plastic card with her photograph on it, and another plastic card with holes in which you fed into the Clock.

They got someone to come in to the dog, but Micah still thought at first,

'Maybe he's lonely,' as she watched the shells of chocolate winding towards her on the machine.

Micah wasn't lonely. She wasn't alone for a moment. Not from the moment she went through the factory gates and put her card in the Clock, to when she came out again and hurried across the concrete yard and got into the queue for the bus and stood waiting for it, in the rain.

It always seemed to be raining. Occasionally it had stopped by the time she got off the bus, but she didn't enjoy the reflections of the houses in the pools of rainwater as she had formerly done. Her head was full of everything that had happened during the day. Sometimes her head felt too full. She wondered if it might split, she was afraid it would, like she had been afraid the turkey would split the previous Christmas when her mother put it in the oven.

'Stuffed fit t' bust!' her mother had said.

But her head didn't split. She spent most of her days in a kind of trance, watching the silvery nozzle it was her job to guard injecting the chocolate moulds with sweet creamy filling. She smelt constantly of peppermint. Her breath reeked of it.

The sweet chocolatey smell never left her nose. Her mother made jokes about it. One of the men came and stood by her in the dinner queue and called her peppermint. She had tied her hair back with a pale green ribbon. The man offered to carry her plate to a table, and as he did so his hand touched her arm.

She didn't have time to go into her head anymore. She tried it once but the Supervisor (who was a fat fair woman in a tight white coat) told her off.

'You better watch yourself, Micah,' she said. 'We got no time for dreamers in here.'

After that, whenever Micah felt herself begin the descent into her head, she deliberately paid attention to what was happening around her.

'How y' getting on?' her mother asked when she got home.

'Oh. It's not bad,' she would say, and begin helping her mother get the tea. In the evenings they watched television without saying anything. Micah's mother usually went to sleep. Micah did sometimes. She bought her mother a new coat and skirt, and some shoes for herself, but didn't wear them. The dog went back to the RSPCA, and for a week the house felt empty.

At Christmas the factory closed and Micah felt restless. She didn't know what to do with herself after she'd eaten the turkey and dutifully sat with her mother and watched the Queen. She moved about the house, bothered by how quiet it was.

She was glad to get to the factory gates again, to go in through the big swing doors and hang her coat up in her own locker and take her customary seat at her machine. People greeted her.

'Well, Micah. How y' doing?'

People called across to each other and joked about Christmas as the first chocolates rolled towards them, and said what they'd got as presents, and said how many drinks they'd had, and who'd been sick.

At dinner time the man who had carried her plate came and stood by her again. That afternoon as she sat at her machine the women teased her about him. She felt pleased but ashamed.

That night she made sure she was on her own as she crossed the yard on her way to wait for the bus. It was very cold, well below freezing, and her ears and her fingers tingled. The street lamps made everything yellow as she walked along the pavement under the factory wall. How strange the shadow of the wall was, dense and reddish after the yellowy light, and her footsteps echoed along the edge of the shadow and the sound of them entered her head.

'Micah!'

She blinked and looked around and saw the man running after her. He was breathing heavily and each breath curled out of his mouth in a big billowy circle which disappeared almost at once.

'I wanted t' catch you,' he said.

Micah just looked at him but didn't say anything. They were standing quite close to the wall, half in streetlight, half in shadow. Micah thought how strange the man looked, as though he was split in two.

He said,

'I bought you a present. Like, for Christmas, y'know,' and handed her a flattish box covered in Christmas paper, holly leaves and berries and pealing bells, but all entirely bereft of colour, reduced to a uniform brownish hue.

'That's what the lights do,' she said. 'Take the colour out of things.'

'Aren't y' goin t' open it?' he said, and took her by the elbow and walked her around the comer away from the bus stop, out of sight of the people waiting there.

'I bought 'em,' he said as Micah took off the paper. 'They're not, y'know, from here or anything.'

Micah said,

'Oh. Yeah. Chocolates. Ta. Them's me favourites.'

Then Micah stood on one leg, awkwardly, not knowing what to do with herself or the big shiny box of chocolates with a single, black-looking rose adrift on the lid. She began to say,

'Look, me bus – '

But at precisely the same time the man put his hand on her wrist and said,

'Won't y' come out tonight? We could go somewhere. Y'know. Have some fun, and that.'

Micah's bus went by quite full up, and Micah was vaguely aware of the brightly lit windows and the dark shapes of people's faces. She thought she saw Imelda waving at her from the top deck. The man gripped her hand, and despite the fact that she didn't much like the strange, hard feel of his fingers, she said,

'Yeah. Alright. Why not?'

FENCING

Coming out of the garden, Eleanor met him. He was moving between the high walls on either side like a grey shadow. He was hatless, and his hands were suspended rather palely from the cuffs of his coat.

Eleanor thought,

'Where is he going?' because the road didn't lead anywhere, and stepped out to ask if he wanted directions. But something about him stopped her, he looked very white, very tired, and rather untidy, as if he had recently become a tramp. How strange his feet looked, because his shoes were odd! And one of the shoes was dark, with white laces. Eleanor looked at her own shoes which were pinkish and made of soft leather and done up neatly.

She thought she ought to offer him a drink, and said,

'Would you like a drink?' and was on the whole surprised when he accepted.

He looked out of place, sitting on the wooden stool in the corner of her kitchen. His hand shook as he took the mug from her. He seemed very tense. But when he began to talk he seemed quite normal, like anybody you might meet, not that she met many people these days, she lived so quietly.

And seeing him sitting there, and hearing him talk in a low voice, drinking occasionally from the mug, attaching his lips to the rim of the mug, disturbing the steady rise of the steam from the surface of the creamy-looking tea so that it shifted sideways and curled over his top lip and up towards his nostrils like the wispy beginnings of a colourless moustache – all this was very pleasant. She would have liked to think that he reminded her of someone, but he was quite unlike anyone she had met before.

He told her that he came originally from America, and his family had been, way back, Scotch-Irish. Eleanor didn't believe him despite the odd, soft, vaguely trans-atlantic way he spoke, but she didn't interrupt, she liked hearing him speak.

'Yes,' he said, 'My mother came out from County Cork in the 1920s. My mother. Now there was a woman.'

Eleanor didn't ask him anything. She would have liked to know why she admired his mother, but she didn't want to interrupt him, she wanted him to go on.

'Yes,' he said again, 'a fine woman. But of course, she died.' He shifted his weight on the stool and sat up straighter and put the cup down on the sideboard, and all these movements disturbed the general calm of the room, and the air whirled about uncertainly and didn't know which rhythm to settle into, and Eleanor saw how the light which came in through the window overlooking the fields came in at an acute angle and stopped just short of the man's feet, in a mottled patch of shadow.

Eleanor wondered if she should ask what the woman died of, but the man's words stood on their own, had already, it seemed to Eleanor, built themselves into a monument which dominated the room. They sat for a minute in silence. Eleanor warmed the palms of her hands on her mug. The steam from her mug rose slowly towards the ceiling, in a straight line.

'Now there's something,' the man said, 'when somebody dies. Have you ever killed a chicken?'

Eleanor shook her head. She didn't like killing things. She felt guilty when she stepped on anything. It was dreadful, stepping on something and crushing it and the insides, so bloody or so colourless, sticking to the sole of your shoe.

'No?' the man said, looking at her fully for the first time, it was surprising how bright his eyes were, how the irises looked dense against the whites, which were slightly creamy and impenetrable.

'No. I don't suppose you would have. A woman like you. My mother used to kill chickens. At the bottom of the garden. She'd slip a carving knife down their gullets. At dusk, usually. You couldn't see them looking at you.'

Eleanor got up and opened the kitchen window about an inch. The kitchen had been very silent, except for the man's voice, and the silence had made his voice seem like an intrusion, but now the outside came into the kitchen through the opened inch of window, and it surprised Eleanor by sounding like the subdued hum of some vast machine, all the sound blended in together, the keys meshed and the edges of the sounds accommodated each other, the wind, the trees creaking, the grass easing itself to the shifting direction of the wind, the indiscriminate twitter of birds, except for one persistent chaffinch whose repetitive singing punctuated the near air and sawed at the treble nerves of Eleanor's ear.

'That's how it used to sound,' the man said. 'Quite like that. But more evening-y. You know what I mean?'

Eleanor nodded.

'Yes. Evening-y. I like the evening. Do you like the evening?' Eleanor nodded. She thought what white hands the man had. She liked men's hands. She put her own hand up to her cheek and smoothed back a piece of hair.

'You live alone here? Don't you get lonely?'

Eleanor was going to answer but the man was looking around the kitchen as if his mind had already moved forward to something else.

'My mother lived alone. She didn't like it very much. She would rather have lived with someone. Wouldn't you rather live with someone?'

He was looking at her again now, with the full, impenetrable look. Eleanor expected to feel uncomfortable, but did not.

'Well. Living with someone. It's not always so good.' The man answered himself.

'You get to bickering. Doesn't matter if it's men or women. Bickering. And then there's the question of yourself. All the accommodating. You get to wondering in the end if there's anything left of you.'

He looked down at his hands. He seemed to be studying them as if they belonged to somebody else.

'But I wouldn't keep chickens. It's the killing. The killing's really something else.'

He had finished his tea, tipped the mug right up and drunk the last dregs, and his raised elbow looked black and angular silhouetted against the window. Eleanor got up and poured him more without asking whether he wanted it.

'But you'd be good for someone,' he said as he took the full mug in both hands. 'Everyone's good for someone. Even I've been good for someone, in my time. But it doesn't last, that's the thing with it. Doesn't last.'

He shook his head and looked out of the window and said, 'Well. And your fence needs mending. I suppose you get someone in?'

Eleanor nodded. She was sitting with her back straight and her hands clasped in her lap. She remembered sitting like that at school services, when she was too young to take Communion. She would wear white ankle socks and black shoes and sit with her ankles crossed and her knees apart, and watch with a kind of dumb awe the brilliant pieces of light which made a mosaic on the altar, sunlight filtering the azure robes of Angels and the bloody skull of the thorn-crowned, dying Christ.

'And what if I was to fix it for you? It'd take maybe half a day. We could come to some arrangement.'

Eleanor said he could mend the fence and watched him working on it through the afternoon. He took off his darkish jacket and under it he had on a creamy shirt. The shirt was too short for him and as he moved it came out of the waistband of his trousers, and as he bent and straightened she saw intermittently the knots of his backbone exposed.

By the time it got dark, he had still not finished the fence. She looked out of the kitchen window just as the sun went down and saw him silhouetted against the fence, whose edges were trimmed with red now, as though the whole had suddenly caught fire. The man himself, his hair and the crests of his arms – everything seemed to have caught fire.

It was a very red sunset. The kitchen was filled with the redness of it as they sat together at the table and ate. It was strange to see him eat. Later, when she showed him to the bedroom, which was set apart from hers across the landing where the house made an 'L', the sight of him there made everything strange. Her plain white curtains looked ridiculous. Her dried flowers in their terracotta pot seemed absurd.

She lay on her bed and listened to him using the shower and waited for the moon to rise and thought she would never get to sleep. After a while she felt her skin chill and took off her clothes and got under the covers and the sheets felt too cool against her skin. It was impossible to get her pillow into the right position.

Once in the night she woke, thinking she heard a floorboard creak on the landing, but although she listened and listened she heard nothing more, and decided it was just one of those night noises you get in a house which is gradually cooling down after a hot day.

She wanted to dream. She nearly always dreamed. Sometimes the dreams were so vivid they made her actual life seem lacking. But tonight, though she wanted to dream, nothing would disturb the insistent blankness of her mind.

When she woke up she felt very disappointed. The patchwork counterpane on her bed was perfectly in place. The day was pale grey, with a high skein of cloud.

She had half a suspicion that the man would have gone. When she went downstairs the place seemed terribly empty. But when she looked in his room he was still in bed, not asleep, but lying on his side under the sheet, blinking slowly as if he were thinking, looking at nothing but the wall. The single sheet emphasized his thinness. She could make out the bones of his shoulders, and the bony sweep where the ribs begin. His thigh, in outline, was curiously like a child's thigh, angular and not much substance to it. When she asked him if he wanted breakfast he said,

'No. I've never been much of a one for breakfast,' and turned onto his back and stretched and flung his arm out on the pillow so that the white underskin of it showed.

It was quite some time before he came down into the kitchen. He took the tea she offered him and went outside to finish off the fence. He kept his jacket on this morning, the air was so much colder.

In about an hour, the whole thing was finished. Eleanor went out to inspect it, and he showed her how taut the wire was over the top of the posts, taking her hand and putting her fingers in between the barbs so she could feel for herself. Touching him was unexpected. It confused her, and she stepped back quickly, and retreated into the house.

The man took a long time to tidy up. She watched him from the kitchen, pretending to do the usual things but unable to concentrate, moving restlessly from one thing to the next, the back of her neck felt tense and she frequently rubbed it, and flexed the muscles by nodding and shaking her head.

The fence was really complete. The new stakes and the shiny new wire stood out against the rest, which had weathered. She knew she ought to be pleased, and yet she felt ambivalent. The man came in and said,

'Well. There's your fence. It's a solid job,' and washed his hands and forearms at the sink, and made a lot of lather with the soap which he didn't entirely rinse away, but left decorating the sink, like the spume an ebb tide leaves after a storm at sea.

When he went, it was unexpected. She had thought he might ask whether there were any more jobs. He took the envelope with the money, and tore it open carelessly with the side of his thumb, and counted out the money on her kitchen table, and folded the notes around the coins in a tight, square packet, and put the packet down into the bottom of his trouser pocket, and left the ragged envelope in the middle of the empty table.

The bag of sandwiches she'd given him made an ugly bulge in his jacket. He looked somewhat less thin as she watched him walk away from the gate, and down the road between the tall grey walls.

She went back into the kitchen, in which the smell of him was barely detectable, and saw that the window was still open about an inch, and wondered whether she should shut it, but decided to leave it as it was, for the time being at least.

L'HOTEL DES GRANDS HOMMES

L'Hotel des Grands Hommes is an ordinary looking little French hotel on the far side of the Place du Panthéon. Three well-scrubbed steps lead up to it. Flanking the steps are two identical fir trees in white wooden boxes, so green and so identical you might doubt they were real except for the moist squares of well-turned earth in which each is planted, a rich dark red, particularly in the evenings when the sun slews down over L'Église de la Sorbonne and the whole square is filled with subdued ruby.

The hotel gets its name from the domed and decaying grandeur of the Panthéon itself, in which are housed the remains of famous men, of Hugo, Zola and the inimitable Voltaire. But one cannot say, though the hotel brochure claims it, that the best rooms overlook the Panthéon. All you can see from your window is a flat expanse of dressed stone, pale ochre in the early mornings, orange at midday, and the gangs of local children roller-skating on the pavement, with patches on the backsides of their trousers and an abundance of unkempt hair.

Marsha and Tony were staying in the Hotel des Grands Hommes by accident. Marsha had found it in a guide book she'd picked up at the *Bureau de Tourisme*, and was attracted by the. name, and the fact that it was situated in the *cinquième*. They'd both wanted to get away from the *huitième* which was beginning to seem just a little pretentious now that Summer was coming and the real Parisiennes were making way for the tourists and you heard almost entirely American voices as you strolled, occasionally checking your reflection, past the elegant windows of the Rue Faubourg St Honoré.

The move made them slightly uncomfortable at first. The *cinquième* is very different from the *huitième* and they needed time to adjust. It was difficult to know what to wear. But perhaps they would have been uncomfortable anywhere. They had come to Paris for a holiday but also because there were things between them which needed to be seen to. They thought it would be easier to discuss in a foreign city those things it seemed impossible to contemplate at home.

Marsha and Tony were no longer in love. Perhaps they had never been in love. Perhaps love did not exist. Perhaps the only thing that existed was philosophy. You could tell they didn't love each other. He kept away from her and her movements, when she inadvertently got near him, were unnatural and stiff.

They were a prosperous looking couple, in a middle of the road way. They had recently made money and he was very involved in his business. She had that dissatisfied look that comes to some women. When they were in a restaurant he sat with his back to the room and she looked past him and generally they left early and walked through the dusk without talking, taking the long way back to the hotel.

On their third morning, the sun rose very gold over the dome of the Panthéon. They were late getting down to breakfast. Marsha had been slow in the shower and Tony had wanted to finish the final chapter of *Thérèse Raquin*. He rather liked the book. His view was, old Zola could put together a good story. That Thérèse. She was really something. But the parts about passion were well portrayed.

They took the lift all the way down to the vaulted basement where breakfast was served, and tried not to look at each other in the mirrors which covered the inside of the lift. As they got out of the lift Tony thought that Marsha was still a good looking woman. Marsha thought this morning they ought to talk. They sat down to their croissants in silence and felt uncomfortable in the empty room.

They began talking about Zola but it was difficult because Marsha didn't know *Thérèse Raquin*.

'There are some real brutish bits,' said Tony, putting a lot of butter on his croissant. Marsha had read *Germinal* and gave her opinion that Zola had a tendency to go over the top. A wrangle began between them, of no very great significance. Marsha was spirited in her own defence. She wrote a little, and had plans to produce the Great English Novel. She'd thought about taking a villa for a month. She knew that was what you had to do. Writers needed space. Maybe she'd take a villa at the end of this Paris thing. She shushed her husband who was talking too loudly and waving his hands. He held a piece of croissant in one hand and waved it in front of her. She told him they weren't alone and he quietened down. Two men were breakfasting behind one of the pillars. Marsha thought,

'Well, now we *can't* talk,' and was relieved. Tony began listening to the men's conversation in a quite uninhibited way. He pushed away his plate and lit a cigarette and pushed his chair back from the table. He asked the waitress in very bad French for more coffee. She brought it grudgingly, which annoyed him. The two men were American and one was interviewing the other. He listened for a few minutes, nodded a couple of times, pursed his lips, drank more coffee, and soon stopped listening, or listened only partially because half his mind was back home, and thinking about his business, and wondering how he could make sure his order books stayed full.

Marsha was in seventh heaven. When she thought about it afterwards going up in the lift she could hardly believe her luck.

'But didn't you recognize him?' she said to her husband, her voice pitching and tossing like a boat on a swollen sea. 'I mean, didn't you hear? Weren't you listening, for God's sake?'

She made a strange little noise when Tony said he hadn't been listening particularly. It was a little snorting noise, somewhere between incredulity and contempt.

'It was Carver, for God's sake. *Raymond Carver!* A real, live writer. Everyone's read Carver. My God, if only you'd listened! You can really learn something, listening to a man like that.'

Tony pooh-poohed it saying what could Carver tell him that he didn't already know? But underneath he was annoyed. You couldn't often listen in on what somebody famous was saying. Marsha kept referring to it. They toured the Musée de l'Orangerie because Tony said it was small enough to get around, and right in front of Picasso's *L'Etreinte* Marsha said again,

'That Carver. The things he said about chaos. You'd be surprised.'

That night she told her husband she was going to take a villa straight after Paris. Nothing very much. Not too expensive. Something simple up in the hills. They spent the evening in because Tony had some calls to make. He needed to call America. Lack of progress on some deals there was scaring him. Marsha sat at a table in the corner and got out a pencil and paper and tried to write. It was some months since she'd written anything and the pencil felt odd in her fingers and the empty pages gave her a stretched feeling in her head. She thought she'd write a story, maybe call it *L'HOTEL DES GRANDS HOMMES*. It was a good title. If she handled it right, she could make it reverberate. She started it several times but it didn't sound right. She sat gripping the pencil and stared out into the courtyard. They had a bedroom which looked out over a small square courtyard. The courtyard was enclosed on all sides, seven stories high. Across the courtyard, on the same level she was, someone was playing Brahms. The piano tinkled as if it were slightly out of tune. Marsha heard traffic revving in the distance and felt claustrophobic. She thought about how it would be when she was really writing. She'd sit by an open window on a terrace with the sun coming slowly towards her, eating up the shade. She wasn't sure what she'd write about. But that would come. There were so many things to write about. 'Order trembling at the edge of chaos.' Had Carver said that? She remembered it from somewhere. She felt happier than she had in a long time. There was so *much* to write about. She understood about chaos. She could write about chaos. As long as she was writing about it she could conquer chaos and be strong.

Tony finished on the telephone and asked if she wanted to go for a drink, but she said no. The next morning she got up early and spent an hour on *L'HOTEL DES GRANDS HOMMES*. Then Tony woke up and got out of bed and farted on his way to the bathroom and Marsha thought how white his body was, and decided not to write any more for the time being.

At breakfast the waitress was affable and Tony seemed good humoured. Carver was there on his own. He sat very still with his coffee in front of him and his shoulders hunched, staring at the table cloth.

'Why don't you go up and introduce yourself?' Tony said. 'You know – writer to writer.'

He said it just loud enough so that Carver would have heard if he'd been listening. But Carver gave no sign, and Marsha shushed her husband angrily. Later she wondered what it would be like to introduce herself to Carver. Maybe she'd do it. There wasn't any reason why not. And yet, when you got down to it, you couldn't possibly do it, not just like that, not go and introduce yourself out of the blue.

She didn't see Carver again that day. But the idea of introducing herself to him stayed in her head. It stayed with her while she and Tony went around the Panthéon. They could only go around part of it because it had been crumbling since the beginning of the century, and was in a bad state of repair.

'We could go up,' Tony said to her. 'There's supposed to be a great view from the walkway that goes round the outside of the dome. You can see everything. There's a great view of Paris. You can even see the Eiffel Tower. And I hear there's a tremendous perspective of Notre Dame.'

She liked the view of the city with its endlessly overlapping roofs. There was something perversely medieval about the tall eighteenth century houses and the ramshackle roofs. When the sun hit the roofs you could see it shimmering off again and everything was very white, there was a white behind the colours of things which was stronger than the colours themselves. In the streets where the sun couldn't get to, everything looked black in comparison. The window boxes punctuating this expanse of white and blackness looked like something which had been spilled.

'There's the Hotel,' she said to Tony, glad to have spotted it and in doing so to have got her bearings.

'I wonder if we can see our room? I don't suppose so. It's on the other side. I left our curtain not quite pulled back.'

They had to climb some narrow steps to get to the upper walkway. Marsha was afraid of heights, especially when you were exposed, and she held onto her husband's arm. He said,

'Don't look down. You'll make it,' and let go of her as soon as they got onto the walkway. She didn't like the city quite as much this time. The view was too high. Everything took on a miniature look which unsettled her. The wind came from across the city in a shifting way.

She moved from pillar to pillar, stopping a little in the protection of each one. They soon went down.

It was a long way down. The crypt was cool and the soft lights made it difficult for her to see after the intense directness of everything outside. That white colour in the roofs. That had been intense. Quite a few people were in the crypt and their footsteps echoed on the stone making a geometric sound. She stopped and bent down to look at the inscriptions next to each stone compartment. You could look through into the compartments where a piece of glass was set into the wall. Tony wandered off somewhere. In one compartment they'd put Zola and Hugo. She was surprised. She wouldn't have thought Zola and Hugo would have sat all that well together. Zola's stone coffin had nothing on it. Hugo's had a flag and a letter and some dried flowers. It looked rather ornate. She was drawn back to look at that compartment again on the way out. Some of the others didn't interest her as much. There were a lot of dead Generals.

From somewhere they were piping through profound music. It sounded like Wagner but she wasn't sufficiently into Wagner to say. On the way out was a benign statue of Voltaire. The wall plaque next to it seemed to be trying to make out that Voltaire was a defender of Catholicism. She said,

'Hey, Tony,' and Tony came round from the back of Voltaire where he'd been intrigued by the effect the fall of his cloak had, it was really amazing how those guys could make things out of stone.

'Hey Tony. You know. This is crazy. Remember *Candide*? Was Voltaire an atheist or *was* he?'

Tony was in a fooling kind of mood, and struck up an attitude. It annoyed Marsha.

'Don't you remember how it ends?' she persisted. '*We should go and work in the garden.*'

Tony shrugged and said, 'Well. Maybe they got it wrong.'

A blue-jacketed official walked by and looked at them queerly. Marsha turned to Tony to tell him they ought to be going but he had wandered off.

The Wagner had stopped and Marsha became aware of how quiet everything was. A few people were still moving about the crypt, like bluish-looking shadows. Voltaire's benignity disturbed her. Surely you couldn't get it wrong about your own hero. Perhaps he had been a defender of Catholicism after all. Perhaps he hadn't been an atheist. She could understand that. You had to believe in something.

She decided, quite suddenly, that she would introduce herself to Carver. There was something about Carver. Tony came up to her again and took her arm and together they left the cool gloom of the hallway and went out into the bright sunshine. As they walked along, Marsha found the thought that she would introduce herself to Carver a consoling one.

Next morning Marsha and Tony woke up on opposite sides of the bed. They'd been out to a bad Italian restaurant and got rather drunk, and on the way back to the hotel they'd quarrelled. Marsha, making erratic progress from streetlight to streetlight, appealed for support to the darkness which was fixed over the city like a dome.

'I *ask* y',' she said, the edges of her voice rather husky.

'*You* ask me? You ask *me!*' Tony was at the gesturing stage. The quarrel had started over nothing, in the restaurant.

'Oh,' said Marsha. 'Oh.' She didn't know why she said 'oh'. She said 'oh' out of a sense, way out on a limb away from every other sense, of something cataclysmic. Her mouth made a little impregnable circle when she said it.

When they got back to the hotel Tony came out of the bathroom with a hard-on and Marsha pretended to be asleep. Sometime in the night, probably about three or four, Marsha woke up. The drink had worn off and everything seemed very bleak. She lay with her back to her husband, and thought about Carver. Then she thought about *L'HOTEL DES GRANDS HOMMES*. She knew she had to try and finish it before they left the next day. It would be impossible to finish it anywhere else. The atmosphere would be wrong, somehow. She lay awake for a while, feeling panicky, but keeping the panic down by breathing slowly, and opening and closing her hands.

They had a rather silent breakfast in the vaulted chamber. Marsha found the *confiture* too sickly. Carver was nowhere to be seen. Tony told her there wouldn't be time for her to work, they had to leave by 10.30.

'You know we said we'd head off down to Perpignan. Perpignan's a long haul.'

There was an artist down in Perpignan who Marsha had a yen for. She"d bought a little nude of his at the *Marché de Poesie* last time they were in Paris. She'd hung it in her dressing room back home in Baltimore and she looked at it every morning on her way to the shower. The way she'd hung it, the light really picked it out. The little nude had her arms raised, pinning up her hair. There was a lot of tension in her elbows. Sometimes it surprised Marsha she wasn"t actually alive.

Marsha didn't write anything else but applied herself to the packing. By about ten everything was in and Marsha was pinning up the sides of her hair. She asked Tony if he thought it made her look more sophisticated and he said,

'I guess.'

Down in the lobby it took a long time for the clerk to prepare their bill. The Carver party was before them. Marsha nudged Tony and said,

'Look. That must be his wife.'

Carver's wife was about fifty, the same age as Carver, and had long brown hair loose to the waist except where it was held up over her ears with two bright red slides. She was deep in conversation with a young Frenchman. Marsha wondered if he was Carver's publisher. It must be really something to have a foreign publisher. She'd have a foreign publisher one day. The young Frenchman held Carver's wife's hands and they looked at each other and smiled a lot. Carver was sitting in the comer and looking out of the window and smoking. Carver's wife seemed very lively. They went outside and got a stranger to take their photograph. It was Carver's wife's idea. She had to call Carver twice before he'd come. In the end they stood together, the three of them, Carver's wife in the middle with her arms draped over both men's shoulders. It was an instant picture and there was great hilarity when she discovered she'd left her flies undone.

'Oh God!' she squealed. 'Just look at me!'

She planted an excited kiss on the Frenchman's cheek and her lipstick came off and left a red impression there. Carver's wife and the

Frenchman went inside and sat in the comer talking and laughing. Marsha thought, there was only one thing that made a man and a woman talk and laugh like that. Carver stayed leaning in the doorway, looking out over the Place du Panthéon. It was a Saturday morning and there wasn't much traffic. It was a dull day and the Place looked smaller somehow, without the sun. Marsha stood watching Carver and Carver stood watching the Panthéon. Tony paid the bill and said,

'Are you coming, Marsha?'

She said, 'Sure,' and picked up one of the cases and walked with her husband down the hotel steps and over to the car.

'That Carver sure looks miserable.'

'Doesn't he just.'

As Tony unlocked the car Marsha looked round and saw Carver still standing in the doorway. He'd finished his cigarette and his hands were hanging down by his sides. The light reflecting off the side of the Pantheon made his face, especially his cheekbones, look bronze. Marsha felt very strongly she wanted to go over to him. She waved Tony out of the parking space and got into the car. The flags that decorated the upper walkway of the Panthéon lifted in a cross wind then went limp. As the car circled the Place and approached the hotel entrance for the final time, Marsha hoped Carver would still be standing there. But as the two green trees in their neat white boxes came into view she saw, with a disproportionate sense of sorrow, that Carver had gone.

THE HOUSE AT WORLD'S END

Barnabas knew Floyd back in the sixties. Floyd was making his reputation. Barnabas was making it with women. Everyone was making it with women back in the sixties. Barnabas didn't always like making it with women. Sometimes he thought he'd like to make it instead with Floyd.

Barnabas was rich and Floyd wasn't. Floyd was a painter. Everyone knew painters were poor. Barnabas didn't mind Floyd being poor. Sometimes he'd buy him dinner. Floyd had a studio in W11. Barnabas had a flat in Markham Square and a house he didn't very often go to further down the road at World's End. Barnabas was not entirely happy. He'd got married the previous year and felt a sense of responsibility towards his wife.

'Why'd you do it?' Floyd said one day. Barnabas was sitting moodily on a box in the corner of Floyd's studio. Floyd was working on a canvas. He had his back to Barnabas. His shirt was hanging out and a loop of it flapped against the outside of his thigh. Barnabas liked the way it flapped on the outside of his thigh. Floyd said,

'I mean, why? You wouldn't catch me doing it.'

Barnabas didn't answer. He wanted Floyd to go on talking. Floyd had an accent. It was nice the way his tongue curled around the ends of words. Barnabas liked watching how his mouth moved. He said,

'How is it?' And Floyd said,

'Bad.'

And then Floyd put down his brushes and stretched both his arms above his head so the muscles in his shoulders bunched up first of all and then relaxed. Barnabas said,

'Dinner?' And Floyd said,

'No.'

Barnabas walked up Kings Road towards his flat and felt bad about
Floyd. He had wanted Floyd to dine with him. It would have been so
nice to have Floyd sitting on his left or his right hand, or opposite
him. Sometimes Floyd put his two hands flat on the table, palms
down, and the backs of his hands looked brown against the table
cloth. They talked about all sorts of things. You couldn't talk about
all sorts of things to women. Something else always happened when
you were with women. There was something about them that just
got in the way. You couldn't say things. They smiled at you and looked
soft. And when you touched them, they were soft. Your fingers, the
ends of your fingers just seemed to sink into their flesh. Of course,
sometimes it was nice with women. Quite often, it was reasonably
nice with his wife. She would put her arms around him and he would
put the side of his head close up against the underside of her left
breast and listen to her heart beating. Her heart beat very steadily.
That was probably how his mother's heart had sounded when he was
as yet unborn and floating in the waters of her womb. And then
again, women could sit so still. It amazed him sometimes, to see his
wife sitting poised and seemingly oblivious, like someone who was listening to a story being told at the centre of herself. Some of the
pictures of the Virgin Mary were quite like that. There was one in
the Uffizi, he couldn't remember what it was called. He liked the idea
of the Virgin Mary. He liked the way painters always showed her
looking at the baby Jesus Christ.

He thought about Floyd again, and wished they were having
dinner. He didn't want to go back to his flat alone. He felt better when
he was with Floyd. The last time he'd had dinner with Floyd, there
had been a bowl of tulips on the table. A white porcelain bowl, quite
small, with less than a dozen tulips in it, cut off short at the stem.
How fiery those tulips had been. Two shades of pink, with a yellow
stripe in them that showed particularly in the ones that were furthest
open. But then again, he liked the ones that were still closed. Those
closed tulips had stayed in his mind for quite a while after. The very
edges of the petals had been so crenellated and so crushable. He and
Floyd had talked about all sorts of things. Really, the restaurant had

been too smart for Floyd. Barnabas liked dining in the smartest res-
taurants. But Floyd was always ill at ease. Barnabas liked it when
Floyd was ill at ease. It made him feel warm, as though a smile had
started inside him of its own accord. They had talked about art and
life and eternity. Floyd didn't want to be mortal. Floyd had said,

'It's like living in an outgrown cage.'

When Floyd said that, Barnabas could feel the mesh of which the
cage was surely constructed. But he didn't really want to think about
it. Sometimes the things Floyd said were very heavy. And actually,
being mortal was quite a good idea. It gave a certain piquancy to
things that might otherwise lack flavour. Barnabas was beginning to
take a serious interest in food and wine, and gastronomic metaphor
was informing many of his ideas.

After they'd had dinner, Floyd had agreed to come back to his flat.
Barnabas was aware of feeling very tense as he asked the question.
And when Floyd said 'Yes' he still felt tense, and ran for a cab to cover
it. On the way back in the cab he'd sat close to Floyd, afraid all the
time Floyd would notice. But Floyd hadn't noticed, and the warmth
his thigh gave off, so close to Barnabas's thigh in the comer of the
taxi, kept Barnabas in a state of near exaltation.

Of course back at the flat nothing had happened. Barnabas managed to arrange things so that he and Floyd drank Armagnac out of
the same glass. Perhaps his fingers touched Floyd's fingers as he
handed him the glass. He liked to think so. And when Floyd had gone
he felt restless and kept going to the window and coming away from
it again.

But now he was going back to the flat alone. It was strange, how
the prospect of being alone could make you feel. It was strange how
even walking up the street alone made you see things differently. The
buildings were large and dark and the lighted windows looked like
oblongs that had been applied with paint. You couldn't see the sky.
Not really. It didn't matter, because you knew it was there. It was there
behind the streetlights, every one of which suspended itself above
you like an individual moon. Barnabas heard his footsteps following
him. He listened to the space the silence made for itself between his
heel on the pavement and the sound which rose up and evaporated

in the general cacophony of city things. That was the kind of space Floyd painted. It was impossible to say how Floyd could paint a thing like that. But he could, and there it was, and all kinds of other things too, and Barnabas wanted to be Floyd, and possess what Floyd possessed, and possess Floyd too.

When Barnabas let himself into his flat, the scent of women and women's things assailed him. Women smelled entirely unlike men. Even when they were not wearing any scent, they were still scented. Men smelled rounder and more wholesome, you could relax with the way men smelled. Barnabas sometimes lent his flat to women so they could sleep around. It made him feel good. Just then he was lending it to a girl Floyd knew. She was dark and thinnish and Barnabas sometimes didn't like her. Especially he didn't like her when Floyd painted her. Floyd had painted her two or three times in the nude. There was a particular canvas in Floyd's studio in which she was lying on a bed which Barnabas recognized as Floyd's. She was lying with her head back and her shoulders loose and her arms spread out with the palms upwards and the fingers lightly curled. You couldn't tell anything from her expression. It was always difficult to tell anything with women. But Floyd had painted her in minute and voluptuous detail, down even to the little half-moons of dirt under her fingernails. Floyd could not have painted her like that unless he loved her. He'd asked Floyd about it and Floyd had said,

'Yes.' And the way he'd said it, Barnabas had been afraid to ask again.

The smell of the girl was very strong in Barnabas's flat. He went through into the kitchen and saw some cups and dirty glasses and a dead cigarette end floating in the sink. He went back into the sitting room and called out the girl's name. There was a little mewing sound from the direction of the bedroom. Barnabas went to the bedroom and found the girl spreadeagled naked on the bed. She was staring at the ceiling and smiling. Barnabas could see she was high. She saw Barnabas and giggled and waved her arm in a vague invitation.

'Barney, hey, Barney,' she said. It was dark in the bedroom but the light which came in through the doorway was whitish on her hips and shoulders and the underside of her outstretched arm. Barnabas said,

'What is it?' He wanted to go towards her but he didn't want to go. Spreadeagled like that, she looked vulnerable. But she looked repulsive too, she looked like something that lies in wait and strikes as you approach it. The girl said,

'Why don't we, Barney. C'mon. Let's just.'

Barnabas walked slowly over to the bed. The girl caught hold of his hand and placed it palm downwards on the soft skin of her stomach. Her stomach felt very soft under his palm. He could sense through the ends of his fingers her pulse beating somewhere deep. He clenched his fingers and thought he could feel the set of her intestines. The uppermost margin of her pubic hair brushed against the underside of his wrist. He felt within himself something terrible. It was hard to say what. Everything seemed separate from everything else. Light and dark, mind and body, and within his mind the thoughts spread out and separated, each one like a bright world suspended in its own darkness. The girl was solid and separate from the bed and everything else. And yet she seemed too to be part of the bed, part of everything, and everything was made just then from the same substance, the room and the girl and the bed and the curtain were sculpted from the same solid block.

He became aware that his heart was beating very fast. He bent over the girl and kissed her. She tasted strange. Her mouth was soft and strange. She said 'Barnabas' and stretched and relaxed her body on the bed.

Barnabas stood up. He thought he stood up quickly but could not be sure. Perhaps he stood up slowly. The room seemed strange. The light coming in through the doorway was yellow and fluid. The girl was moving her body on the bed but he hardly noticed her. The scent of her pressed up into his nostrils as he left the room. He went out of the flat and down the stairs and into Markham Square. A car swerved past him, going much too fast. Barnabas began to run, steadily at first, with his arms and his legs pumping and his feet hitting the pavement in a measured rhythm. Kings Road opened out before him. He saw the people and the lights and the cars and the shop windows. The sound of it all broke over him and he cringed back into himself. He ran faster and more raggedly, nothing in co-ordination, breath and legs and arms entirely out of tune with each other, until by the time he saw his house, with the light from the hall lying like a mat on the pavement, his lungs were burning and his whole body was trembling as though he had narrowly escaped fate.

He let himself into the house and went upstairs slowly and looked into his bedroom. He could see the outline of his wife on her side of their bed. With just his wife in it, the bed looked curiously empty. Under the cotton cover his wife seemed small. He thought of Floyd. If only Floyd were there. He could talk to Floyd. He closed the door and walked along the landing to an empty bedroom. His wife had chosen the decoration. The light had a pink shade. The shadows that it cast went deep into the corners of the room. 'Floyd,' he said. He lay down on the bed and felt how the mattress shaped itself against him. He wanted Floyd, but he didn't know what that meant, except somehow he was attached to Floyd, Floyd was a piece of himself that he had to get back. He turned the light out and rolled onto his side and felt uncomfortable in his clothes. He heard a sound on the landing and thought it might be his wife. He wondered about going to Floyd. But Floyd was in his studio probably, in the little bedroom next to his studio where Barnabas sometimes sat with him, with the chair and the bed and the lamp and the way the paint smelled. Barnabas shivered and clasped his arms about his chest. He pressed his fingers hard into his ribs. A feeling formed within him that he took to be longing. He sat up suddenly and thought,

'Yes. I'll go!' But just then the landing light came on. He could see it under the door, a bar of hard white light. And he thought to go would be impossible because Floyd would surely be sleeping and W11 was, in any case, much too far away.

LOSING

'But what is it like?' she had asked her mother a long time ago, when she was about eight and a half, the middle of the first year in the new school.

'Really. What is it *like*?'

'Oh. It is nothing. It is just a lot of heavy breathing, really. That is all.'

She had been very much older than her years, even then. Distant relatives who came occasionally and went, wondered among themselves if she had ever really been a child.

'Such a dark, serious girl. And a great pity, when you think of it. But there.'

And this one would smooth the multi-coloured feather at the side of her felt hat, that one would dust off the brim of his trilby with clean, thin fingers going the same way as the nap, and they would move on to other more important issues, the rising cost of living, the encroachment of Socialism, the perils of this (for so they were beginning to think of it) permissive age.

Being very much older than her years even then, she had not made the kind of quick, instinctive reply you might usually get from a child. She waited, saying nothing, watching the nervous movement of her mother's hands straightening and straightening a pair of thick-knitted and unmistakably male socks.

'These came from Aunt Evelyn,' her mother said irrelevantly. 'I don't think she knows his size.'

How she had watched, after, for him to put on the socks for the first time, wondering would they fit, watching as he sat down with them in his hand, the lamp light casting the shadow of the kitchen table partly on him as he pulled off his slippers and lined up his boots, with ice edging the pond like an ageing eye, and snow clouds massing like great grey packs on the back of Arran Fawddwy.

His bare foot shone in the firelight, bronze and pink mixed in together, like sunset was sometimes, very rarely towards the end of Summer when the dew comes down by about eight o'clock and you take in your things quickly and close your front door against the rising silence. She could see in the firelight the hairs growing below the cuffs of his long-legged winter underpants and down onto his instep, black and wiry as briar. Black and bronze and pink and then the sudden sharp detachment of shadow under the muscley arch.

His foot slipped easily into the thick, knitted sock. First the tensed toes into the precise gap held open by his thumbs. Then quickly over instep and arch, stretched round the hard bulb of his heel, then up over the ankle bones he unrolled the rough knitted stuff until it met the edges of his underpants, engulfed them, drove on smoothly another two inches, and he tidied it with a satisfied pat and drew the trouser bottoms down over it all like a blind.

'What are you staring at?' She stepped back into the longish shadow which his body cast.

'Nothing.'

'They fit, then,' said her mother from the corner by the stove, peevishly, as if somehow aggrieved.

He put on his coat and went out without answering. Not until nearly an hour later, when it was entirely light, could the kitchen quite rid itself of the cold blast his opening and closing of the door had let enter.

Winter. Spring. Summer. Autumn. Four arcs on a slowly rolling wheel. When you are nine, or ten, or eleven, the length of each is inordinate. The days seem endless, yet afterwards resemble no more than flakes you could scrape off with the edge of your nail from a healing graze.

When she was nine, she liked Winter best. Everything seemed to have stopped. She liked existing in this limbo, everything in a state of waiting, with the force of it filling up inside, the growing sense of pressure until things gather and give.

When she was ten it was Spring the young lady (for so her mother began to try to tell her she had become) now favoured. '*I like Spring because it is beginning,*' she had written for an English composition and been marked down because it was, so Miss Bristow who did English said, bad grammar. She did not understand. Spring was beginning-transitive and intransitive, verb, noun, adjective, all of it. '*Spring is beginning.*' She couldn't put it into any other words than those. Any other way she tried to describe it sounded flat and lifeless, or else sounded as if someone else was saying it, not her.

'*Summer is icumen in*' was the start of a verse she learned sometime during the dusty season at the centre of her eleventh year. Rainless days turned into weeks. A fine, dry Summer developed into something called drought. *Drouth. Drowt.* She tried out the word over and over, balanced it on the tip of her tongue, dribbled it into the succulent parts of her inner gum, slipped the unfamiliar edges of it painlessly past the supple cordings of her throat. *Drouth. Drowt.*

'*Dammit!*'

The shout in the middle of the night, squeezing up through the floorboards as though the parlour were not big enough to contain it. But coming suddenly awake like that, in the middle of the night, with the moon very white on you, it is sometimes difficult to decide whether it was just a dream.

Her mother saying, 'I do pray for rain'. And the sympathetic superior look of the man who delivered the paraffin as he tilted his head a little to listen and took the funnel out of the ten gallon tank and shook the last few pink drops from it and screwed down the top.

The stream was a not a stream anymore but a sickly trickle. The stones which the water usually flowed over looked dull and lumpish. You could only just hear the movement of it, a little lurking sound, only just audible at the edge of your head. Everywhere was very dusty. As you walked up the track from the road, your heels kicked up fussy little whorls of dust which hung there for quite a while after you had passed. The ground was hard and began cracking. Every day, cracks you had discovered the previous day widened and deepened. The chickens looked thin and stopped squabbling among themselves over who was to take the first dust bath in the comer of the yard.

At night the downstairs light stayed on a long time.

'*Dammit!*'

The dust settled in the creases that lay like straight drains from both his nostrils to the comers of his mouth. When the dust mixed with his sweat, it pasted his hair together in ugly clumps. His hands were black, the collar of his shirt dirty. He began to resemble in part the carelessly constructed thing she and the others humped from farm to farm at the beginning of each November, to the reedy and discordant chorus,

'A penny for the guy! *Ceiniog. Ceiniog.*'

In her eleventh year, she certainly liked Summer best. Short, hot nights. Blurred moons which cast the pointed shadow of the pine across her as she lay in bed. The dusty, acrid smell of the grass. The thin chickens drawing out sore sounds from the backs of their throats like slowly stretched strings.

It was inevitable that when she was twelve, Autumn would have its tum as her favourite. She was such a sullen and capricious thing.

'What child can like Autumn best?' demanded the departing relatives of themselves, casting the memory of the place firmly over a turned shoulder, shuddering a little as though a sliver of something had insinuated itself at the root of the heart, and was levering it loose.

Autumn was melancholy. That was why she liked it best.

'*I am of a melancholic humour*' she said to herself, draining Shakespeare at a sitting, waking to some ancient clash of harnesses and kingdoms, falling asleep under the eyeless invigilation of a Lear, dreaming, perhaps, of Cordelia.

'I like leaves that are yellow and red, and the frosted pattern of them.'

There was no stillness that could match the stillness of things when there was absolutely no wind. It was quite different from the stillness of still life, a book you had just put down on the table, a chair that nobody was sitting in, an unattended desk. It was stillness *within which* was movement, like Van Gogh's *Sunflowers*, a print she had recently come across in one of her mother's old books, retrieved from a trunk in the back of the attic. This movement-within-stillness seemed to her to be at its peak in the clear days of early Autumn, when the sun took longer and longer to come up and the turning leaves curled round each other at the edges and dropped like sky divers in a suicide pact to lie on the ground till the frost got them, and her own feet, probably, crushed them into brittle bits.

At thirteen and at fourteen no one season seemed better to her than another. Everything was held together with a sameness, as if a grey lens had been slipped into her retina, there to interpose itself between her and the world like the reflection of a grey veil. Daily, man-made rhythms were of more significance to her than natural, seasonal ones. What occurred day by day made sense. The getting up, the half mile walk to the corner, the lift in Mr Bristow's Land Rover which occasionally contained Miss Bristow and, much less often, Mr Bristow's young and silent wife.

'They keep to themselves,' her mother said, half inquisitive, half critical, as she handed over the carefully counted brown and silver coins which went to pay Mr Bristow for his trouble.

These daily events made sense, and the school routine, the bell every forty minutes, break at eleven fifteen and whispering among the rows of gabardine mackintoshes in the empty cloakroom. Changing for games, stripped to your blue serge bloomers, the wind hitting your chest through your cellular blouse as though you had absolutely nothing on. Writing in your pink preparation book lists of things you had no intention of doing. Then waiting on another corner half a mile from the school gates where there was an old wall and a new seat and a carved stone which said 'Grammar School Repaired 1857'. The stone with its carving jarred just a little every time you passed it. The carving was so sharp and clear, as though someone had only yesterday taken his hammer and chisel out of his bag, got down on his knees and manufactured this brief piece of meaning.

She tried to imagine how it had been over a hundred years ago.

Vague pictures came to her, insinuations. It was as if she were marooned on a tiny island, straining to decipher across a sea of seasons the faint and blurry shape of the shore. A sense of helplessness overcame her. Once when she felt like that Miss Bristow looked at her, but didn't say anything.

At the beginning of the grey time, towards the end of when she was twelve, she was visited by what her mother said was womanhood.

'But I am b-bleeding,' she said with the first trace of that afterwards characteristic stutter.

'It is nothing. You are hardly losing. Here.'

The strangeness soon faded among the pink and white appliances her mother provided. But the revulsion which she felt, a kind of subdued horror at her own fleshliness, kept with her.

'Be sure you don't have anything to do with boys or men,' said her mother, looking at her carefully over a pile of folded clothes.

After that, she steered clear of anything faintly male. The piano master she went to once a week after school, she became even more restrained with. When he bent over her to turn the page of his own score to *Mae Hen W'lad* she shrank back into herself and her fingers faltered on the keys. She didn't like the smell of his breath. He said,

'Well, *Cariad*,' and gave her more scales to practice.

'He breathes very heavy,' she said to her mother, who was mending trousers in the uncertain light of the fire.

'No doubt the poor man has asthma,' said her mother without looking up. 'Don't you think so, Brynmor? That the poor man has asthma?'

He sat with his legs stretched out straight, facing the fire, so his toes seemed in danger of roasting and you could already tell that his thick, knitted socks were yellowing in the heat of it, and the scent of scorching mixed with the heavy yellowy smell of his sweat.

'Ah,' he said. 'It's likely. That pansy. Playing the pianer.' She felt his sneer was for her, and she protested.

'But you *said* I should learn. You *said* it was for the best.'

'Now then.' Her mother's voice hovered above the needle plying silvery tracers along the green seam.

'It's a good thing for a girl, the piano. The piano's a good thing for a girl to learn.'

'I hate it. And I hate *him*; and his b-breathin'.'

'*O-o-o-oww.*'

Miss Bristow was whimpering like a kitten in the corner. Her legs were folded up under her and her face was hidden by her hands and she looked crushed.

Or was it a dream? She tried to decipher some of the little differences which delineate dream from reality. It seemed real enough. She was watching through the window a scene in the Bristow's big kitchen. She had seen Mr Bristow shake his young and silent wife as a cat shakes a rat, until she had run out of the room. She had seen Mr Bristow shake Miss Bristow until she had pleaded and gone limp and whimpered. Miss Bristow had not at first screamed or cried. She had only screamed when Mr Bristow hit her in the stomach. His fist made a soft, thudding sound as it met Miss Bristow's stomach, rather like the sound her mother made, plumping up the pillows when she did the beds.

'Slag!'

Mr Bristow stood over Miss Bristow with his legs apart and his hands hanging down by his sides. He turned to go but as though it were an afterthought, kicked Miss Bristow just where the pelvic girdle hinges with the hard, bony part of the upper thigh. The toe of his boot made a sound like 'slup', but Miss Bristow didn't scream, just twitched like a puppet does when somebody clumsy is trying to manipulate the strings.

She stopped looking in at the window then. She heard a door slam and the sound of his boots as he crossed the yard, a flinty sound, stone against metal stud. She came away from the window as she heard him get nearer, and tried to pretend to herself she had just arrived. His shadow came round the corner before him, flat and black on the stone. Then he appeared like an unnecessary adjunct to the shadow, his very fleshiness somehow unreal, as if you could poke a stick right through it, as if it were matterless.

'Uh?' he said when he saw her.

He seemed the same. Quiet and tidy. You would never have thought there was any harm in him. His hair grew down in a brown wave in front of his ears. She didn't like that. But his hands were clean. He seemed neutral, and his skin, particularly around his mouth and in the middle of his cheeks, was pinkish and neutral. She hadn't really looked at his eyes before, and now that she tried to, they were nondescript.

'Uh?' he said again, but the same as always, nothing friendly or unfriendly.

She held out the packet of twelve bantam's eggs, her mother's offering for something or other, an extra lift.

He said,

'Oh. Ah. *Diolch.*' And took them not roughly, as she had supposed, with a great danger of his big thick fingers poking holes through the thin shells, but in his open palms, gently, the effort of gentleness making his fingers quiver, and his arms right up to the elbow, as he carried them in.

He gave her a lift back because it was on his way. He didn't say anything as they bumped along, nor did she, just held on to the handle half way up the door and watched the white light of midday go by them. When you looked outside at the white light and the sky behind it, then inside at Mr Bristow or your feet or the gearstick or the floor, your eyes took time to adjust, and everything seemed black and white like a photograph, but more like a negative, where you couldn't really tell who was who, only by outline, and people's hair was white and their faces black and their mouths white so you had to guess their expression.

Mr Bristow's hand looked black. It looked like a black predatory thing, a giant spider or a great black bat as he moved it around the cab, up to scratch the side of his nose, down to change gear, back onto the steering wheel which bucked and shuddered as they went over the holes in the road. She hated his great black hand. The cab got smaller and smaller, the hand bigger still, his nose and his jaw seemed to elongate, his body got squatter, and his deep, even breathing deafened her. When she looked out the sky and the mountain around her which rose and fell like a great green sea, hinged and tilted. She thought,

'I must stop this. I must get out,' but could do nothing to accomplish it.

They went on like that for another mile. Just when she could feel something about to give, he yanked on the handbrake and they stopped. He didn't look at her as she climbed down, just muttered something. As soon as she had slammed the door the Land Rover began to move, and before she had walked more than a dozen steps it was out of sight.

The smell of half burned petrol wafted up into her nose and she shied away from it. She could hear the sound of the engine getting fainter as it went down the hill. She crossed the road and walked towards the gate. A buzzard swung into the edge of her vision and hung there like a mobile over a child's cot. She heard it mewing, a high sound, rather like a child. A raven came grunting over the pink tip of Tir Stent and flapped slowly towards the North. A south-west wind made a sucking sound in an old roll of wire. The wind in the grass went wuush, shuush, and rattled the gate in her hand as she opened and closed it. It was a white, high, blowsy, April day. Everything seemed to be running in front of itself, there was no stillness anywhere, her hair whipped and jiggled about her ears and onto her cheekbones. She felt for the first time a sense of herself in relation to everything else, as if she were part of a single system, a fragment of something hurrying towards its own special destiny. She put her hands on the top bar of the gate and looked out over the long horizon, clean and green and very definite at the edges.

She turned and began walking up the track. Her skirt lifted and billowed in the wind. She felt a sudden cramp in the lower part of her stomach, right at the front and just above the mons veneris whose identity she had looked up in a school biology primer, and which stuck out in trousers. She recognised the symptom and was not surprised when, within a minute, she felt the first tickling in the cotton gusset of her knickers. She fumbled in her pocket and discovered a grubby paper handkerchief which she stuffed in past her knicker elastic under the pretence of bending down to do up her shoe. She felt like crying but didn't, just kept on up the track towards the house which got bigger and bigger, dwarfing the mountain behind and filling up her whole view. She noticed she was clenching and unclenching her hands, first right then left, rhythmically, in time with her steps to which in turn she controlled and slowed her breathing.

As she neared the house she heard the explosive *phut* of the axe settling its head into a block of wood. Then again *phut* every few seconds as the axe split block after block. *Phut* step step step. *Phut* step step step. She felt like a piece of a machine, something self regulating and contained, and the sound of the axe and her steps and her breathing filled her head until she thought she would never hear anything else ever again.

She entered the yard and walked towards the house. As she approached the kitchen door she saw with unrepeatable clarity its every detail, how the paint was peeling a bit down the one side, little green flakes quivering in the wind, how black and shiny the latch was from a recent cleaning, how bright the hinges looked because they had only been replaced the month before, and just as she saw these things, as they fell into her head as notes do in a musical composition, the door opened and her mother stood back, waiting for her to go in.

SECOND BELL

'Well. Alright. Alright,' said Suluki. 'What d'you want me to do?'

She had very smooth skin and amber eyes set slightly apart, and I had no idea what I wanted her to do.

'Come with me to the shrubbery and play something.'

I yanked at the knot of my girdle, making it look untidier than ever, and tried to adjust the pleats of my gabardine gymslip. Suluki always looked so neat. I always looked as if my clothes had been thrown on. I suppose it was something to do with the way we were made. Suluki got prizes for deportment. I was always getting told not to slouch.

'Well. OK. Just for a bit.'

Suluki had a brand new watch which her father had given her for Christmas, a neat circle of gold with discreet dots where the numbers should have been, and a shiny looking brown leather strap. She consulted it now, just a little ostentatiously, a slight frown wrinkling the skin between her eyebrows and above the bridge of her nose, a frown which hinted at more pressing matters, at very little time to spare.

'There's still ten minutes to second bell,' I said, hearing how the words sounded in my head, how they must have sounded to Suluki, brittle and nonchalant and pleading and creepy.

'Alright, alright. I said I will.'

She followed me out of the side door, refusing to shudder as I did when we stepped from the shelter of the high stone building and the wind cut through our twin navy pullovers with the School colours clustering close around the V-necks, and slid under the meagre protection of our ties, mine maroon, hers white and navy because we belonged to different Houses, and pinched at the flesh stretched thinly over our collarbones.

'What d'you think you're doing?' called a Prefect from the other side of Top Terrace. 'Go back and get your coats!' Suluki looked at me and I looked at her. The Prefect was too far away. We only knew she was a Prefect by the way the light flashed off her silver badge, long short, long short, like the beginning of a message in morse code.

Without saying anything we dodged around the corner and trotted past the netball courts towards the large semi-circle of tended grass in whose centre was the shrubbery rose, green and broad leaved and faintly mysterious and smelling, as it always did, sweet with decayed vegetation.

I crossed my arms over my chest and kicked out my heels and wondered about Suluki. I did not know what to do with her. We never went around together. Suluki's best friend was absent. I didn't have what you might call a best friend. I went around with people when they were free. It seemed that nobody was free this lunchtime, and Suluki and I had come across each other by default.

I'd noticed her before, of course. We all had. She was different. She was rather pretty and had a single, black shiny plait which hung down the middle of her back and bounced and jiggled like a mad, black snake when she ran. She was clever, too. It was difficult not to watch her as she deftly wielded compasses and set square, frowning down at a clean sheet of graph paper, making pencil notations in the right hand margin, hunching over the growing calculation, unaware of how the rest of us groaned and shifted and whispered and congealed in the mess of our own incomprehension. Her shoes were shiny and she always had a clean handkerchief in her tunic pocket. She usually came top. Once I had told my mother about her. My mother didn't say anything, just nodded and looked. Then later on, maybe a day or two later, she said,

'I had a friend like that once. Her name was Muriel. She married young.'

I thought of my mother saying that now, as we entered the green, secret gloom of the shrubbery, ducking under the fat, silver limb of some unnamed species, coming upright again in a leafless, trunkless space among the leaves and trunks, where the earth was absolutely flat and unaccountably smooth, as though a diligent housewife had wielded her broom and swept it clean.

'It's a bit like a dinner plate,' I said, 'a dinner plate just washed clean.'

Suluki broke off a twig and held it between her fingers and broke it again and dropped it onto the ground. I don't know what it looked like lying there, almost exactly in the middle of the dinner-plate space. Like something broken. Like something that was alive and is now dead. Like somebody's leg that has been blown off in an explosion.

'Well?' she said.

I shuffled my feet and shifted about. I didn't know what to say. I was very cold and my fingers were beginning to turn blue. I knew my nose was getting very red on the end. It always did when I got too cold. Suluki just looked herself.

She reached up for another twig and broke it off but this time it wouldn't come away cleanly, she had to twist and twist and wrench and tear, use both her hands to pull it off, it was right at the end of February and the sap must have been beginning to rise and it made this twig, which looked dead enough on the outside, green and sinewy within. Where she had wrenched the twig away was like an untidy amputation. Sinewy bits stuck out at odd angles. Stuff welled up. Suluki had got some of it on her fingers and she must have not liked it, maybe it felt sticky, like blood does, because she tossed the twig over her shoulder straight away, I didn't see where it fell, and got out her clean handkerchief from her tunic pocket and began wiping her fingers individually, each finger from root to tip, with a twist as she did it, very efficiently, just like she did everything else, so that not a drop of the stuff stayed on her skin.

She put the handkerchief away and I could tell she was getting bored from the way she looked around and sucked at her bottom lip and tossed her head so that her shiny black plait jerked and shuddered like a just waking snake. I didn't know what to say to her. I had got her there in a way under false pretences. She expected something and it was all my fault. I have never known what to do when people expect things of me. I still don't. I said,

'I buried something here.'

There was a flicker of interest as she looked at me. Her eyes seemed more almond, more tilted, than they had ever done.

'What sort of thing? Money? Jewellery 'n stuff?'

'N-no.'

'Well?'

She was all curiosity. For the moment I really had her attention. In a way it felt good, like the sun coming out when you don't expect it to. But in another way it felt strange and uncomfortable, like when the sun is out but you can't get any warmth from it, it's a cold sun that seems to pierce you to the bone. I had felt like that once when I was in the Alps and sickening for the *grippe* and nobody realized and everybody thought I was putting it on when my teeth began to chatter and I told them I thought I was going to die with the cold.

'Why didn't you tell us you were ill?' they said afterwards, not quite looking at me, as if they had done something of which they were a bit ashamed. And I hadn't known how to explain that I couldn't explain.

'Is it something you've stolen?'

As I remember it, Suluki licked her lips, and her lips were all pink and shiny where her tongue had passed over them, until the cold air dried them off and they looked dull again, but duller than they had before, with the now dried skimming of whitish spit. But I expect that is something I have added on afterwards, in the nearly thirty years through which I have existed since, swimming to the limits of each one like a fish in the globe of its bowl, searching out the world and discovering nothing but the thin repetition of my own reflection, eyes and mouth and the necessary circuition of jaw.

I said,

'No. It's nothing I've stolen.'

And seeing how her interest began to diminish, added quickly, before I had time to think,

'I buried a bird.'

'What kind of a bird?'

'A dead bird.'

She looked at me speculatively.

'Why dead?'

'I don't know. Just dead.'

She pulled at the end of her long, black plait.

'But what *kind* of?'

I felt hopeless, much as I did in arithmetic tests, when I didn't know the answer, didn't really know what the question meant, wondered at the abyss which came between me and everything around me; teetered on the brink of a great space into which, at any second, I must inevitably fall.

'I don't know what kind. Dead, that's all. Just dead.'

I could feel the gap between us widening. She drew away from me as a big ship does, slowly, gracefully slipping away so the illusion is created of mutual movement, of the courteous manoeuvrings of preordained formality.

'I found it at the end of the Summer Term and buried it. I come every week and put something. A flower or something. I shall do, every week until I leave. Every week for the next ten years.'

She looked at her watch casually, without hurry, then yawned and shook herself. The circle of the watch winked deep and bronze-looking under the canopy of green leaves. Suluki said,

'I don't believe you.'

Just then the bell went, a jangly, arrogant sound which seemed to enter my bones and set me quivering as though my fingers were in contact with the metal and the striker was sending its messages directly down my nerves and into my flesh.

I started to say, no, wait, look, I'll show you, wait a minute and I'll dig it up, it's here, see, right by this root, where this root and that one meet, I'll dig it up and show you what's left, the bones, a bit of flesh maybe, a maggot or two, a single sleek feather with the sun still in it, the black beak through which a remnant of its birdness may still speak. For you I'll dig it up and do these things. Suluki! Suluki!

But she had already turned and ducked out of the shrubbery under the silver limb, was already five feet away, ten, fifteen, I could see the neat set of her shoulders poised over her hips, the thick, black plait swaying gracefully as she walked, the shape that her body was already taking on, like my mother, like all mothers, the same compactness, and the swing of her bottom and her thighs as she walked away from me, never hurrying but covering the ground in a way that was unstoppable, as the tide does when it washes out the shapes that you have made along the shore. And I thought, like Muriel my mother's former friend, Suluki was sure to marry young.

A SMALL STORM OVER PADDINGTON

He had let the flowers die on purpose, she was sure of it.

He has let them die, yes, let them die, but why, why, that is what I do not understand about it.

So it was that she spoke to herself about such matters.

So she had always spoken.

Why did you let them die, she asked him.

He shifted his shoulder round away from her a bit and said, I did not.

What can you do when a man lies to you?

They lie.

And what is the point of words unless they contain within them the weight of truth?

Oh she had married him in haste indeed and now she was repenting, repenting, at a thing called leisure.

Will you come out now, he said to her, big there before her and uneasy.

She paused for a second as if to give the sense of one considering it and then said,

No

He was like a bull, yes, a bull that shakes its head and steps out ponderously with a slow roll of its shoulders and then if you make a sudden movement shies off and gives its horns a shake.

Ah God.

When he came up the stairs at night the weight of him made them creak.

He carried his belly before him like it was something he'd found about him he was obliged to.

Had he ever been young? He was youngish once, he was, for she remembered it. She was younger than he was, much younger, so much younger. She stepped out with a particular quickness. Her hands moved. Her head was on her neck that looked about her, seeing.

I am in the world, she said to herself still, with an amazement. She wanted to cry sometimes, with a kind of joy.

She had married him under one dispensation and lived with him there now under another.

There was a vein in the back of her leg that she had seen, like a blue worm.

Look at this, she said, look. What am I to make of it?

He had sat on the edge of the bed, dumbly.

It was not, the palms of his hands seemed to say to one another, his fault.

The night of the thunderstorm, which must have been about ten years ago, was a night she remembered.

Sometimes you wished you didn't remember things, but there was a smell of sulphur, that much was certain, and the air was blue.

Curiously blue, that was how she remembered the air was. The storm had been there at the edges of things all day. She had gone about the things that she had to do with her head heavy.

He came in.

He put his cap on the peg on the back of the door and the peak of it swung to and fro several times like the disc in the clock in the hall did when it was striking.

He told her there was a storm coming.

She said,

What am I to do about it?

She saw the slow mechanism of his mind working as he turned towards her.

It was the first time she had spoken to him sharply.

He turned his head towards her slowly, in surprise.

And what a rush of something she had felt then, contrition, tenderness, all overlaid with a kind of hatred.

What she felt above anything was the substance of him keeping her in.

I do not want to be kept inside myself like that, she had thought.

I do not want to be confined in these particular boundaries.

His presence was something she wanted to hurl herself up against, like a door.

Later when they had eaten he sat opposite her. There were two small logs burning in the grate although it was a hot evening.

The house was cellar-like.

The smell of the logs burning was pleasant as it trickled into the room.

You could see the lightning flashing occasionally on the horizon.

He sat up suddenly, straight out of his backbone.

That was a big one, he said.

When the rain came, which it did much later, just when it was about to get dark, she remembered she had left the door of the shed wide open.

I had better go out, she said, and shut it.

He half got up and said, I'd better come with you.

She moved her hand up and down with a jerk and said,

No. Don't.

Once I came from a place where it rained on some days and did not rain on others.

The rain came down very straight out of the sky.

It made sense because the clouds that held the blue pan of the sky up off above them were dark and dense.

No sky now was as dark as those had been. No blue so liquid that you kept it in your palm afraid to move and tilt the pool into a spillage that would leak between your fingers, awful magic in its dropping into nothing with never so much as a stain to tell you it had been.

I close the door behind me and those times return.

Is it him?

Not him precisely.

It is words?

Yes. No.

Is it the flowers in their bending over that I can have no remedy towards?

Behind the trees the light of the sky flashes.

It is, so they would tell me, the edges of two clouds that rub against each other.

What storms there would be late in the night with the owl gone silent and the dark sky crushed in on itself as the sides of the world pulled in together.

But then on a calm warm night in summer the waves of it would go like there had never been a thing called a beginning.

It comes like that so that the corn do ripen.

Simple superstition.

The roots of it go deep and blunt like the core of a boil.

The woman crosses the farmyard wholly aware of her way in the thin dark.

The dark you get there, out towards the West, is both complete and incomplete.

It is complete because no human light of city or of town, no string or intersection of the short village street exists, no hidden limit of illumination that the untrained eye is unaware of, no lie which says Look! we can hold back the night!

It is incomplete because the eye becomes accustomed to all shades of dark and can distinguish, even in a seeming perfect blackness, those gradations which defy always and ever the idea of absolute.

In the Summer you can walk out and see the other person's features, how the aspects of him are configured and the way the fingers go back with a little quirky narrowing to the palm.

She pulls the bolt back and lets herself into the stable and what warm smell of flesh comes up towards her skittering with the finger on it and the rough stuff of the mane and tail that you are always just a little bit afraid of lashing gently with a quick shift of the quarters and a shake of the head.

There, now.

Is *this* what it is, this slightly acid smell of the flesh of animal which will one day revert to that unquick edge of something that is no more than a sigh?

He tosses his head back on his neck towards me.

His breath comes out in a hot and wettish little cloud. How is it that I am in the wrong time and place altogether? She smooths his flesh down with the hard part at the heel of her hand that is made of muscle.

In another life, another age, another phase of the moon perhaps, the woman steps down from the train with a bag in her hand.

She pauses, looks about her, signals for a porter.

And now the people come along the platform past her and it could be, for want of some small sleight-of-mind, grass moving under the moon at night, all with an independent rhythm that is yours only to contemplate. Or it could be the sea on that small part of coast that lies below the road and quite away from it where you have walked, or not walked, and where the sun came up and held you there like a mosaic, and your shadow was a static thing.

Once you had thought, as all old-fashioned women do, God, or that which you might call a God-equivalent, might be the answer.

The answer is the flash in the electric cables overhead as the train passes.

The cab pulls out over the sleeping policemen at the station entrance with a sudden jerk.

And this is Paddington, away on all sides like the little blocks of bakelite you had to build things with, there at the base of the green tree with the needles dropping, oh how sharp they were, that stuck in the carpet, and prickled your fingers when you went to dig them out.

The roar that might be of a cosmic waterfall, that is what strikes you. All sound fountains up out of the centre of this manufactured animal and cascades in particles that jostle at each other and rub up the fabric of yourself.

Smooth back your hair.

The cab goes forward. The ghost of a woman – what shall be her name? – rests her cool forehead on the horse's side.

The cabbie is asking whether the journey has been good.

Up there? he says. I went there once. Beautiful. But wet. And at night, you could hear things. The wife was frightened, I can tell you. *Come in out of it*, she said. It was the darkness. We take out the photographs and show them to our friends.

He changes gear, and outside in unison the traffic lurches.

You get to the hotel and the doorman in a jacket whose bright red is not a colour that came out of nature steps up towards you with a high-nosed air. An acrid smell comes up and hits you as the door opens. For a minute it might be the dung of the stable or the round sheep-droppings that lie folded one onto the other slimy with mucous as the mist thickens.

Then you catch your breath and it is traffic only on your tongue and teeth, the slightly grimy taste people and places that are made will always give you.

What is the truth? the woman says with her head on the horse's neck and something crackling along the rim of what it is that she exists within.

The man sits at the table waiting. He stretches slowly, with his arms high up above his head, picks up the matches and a flare bears witness to the lighting of his pipe.

Some time later, whether it is a year, or ten, or the space of an Autumn afternoon spent on some pressing business in a hotel near Paddington with flags outside it which, in this present air, hang with no movement, you emerge.

Breathe deeply. You are alive. Around, all movement, all the shifting things of signs and cities call to you to come.

Will you heed them as the sailors did the Sirens?

The streets are garish and the sky above them puffed out with light.

The scent of a familiar life that is made up of time and disappointment takes you in as you first turn the key and then remove it.

The light when you go in the room seems at first to have that savage element that you get on a winter hillside with the bracken dying. It is the neon sign across the street, reflected.

Books and newspapers and silken curtains and the picture you brought with you.

He comes out of the bedroom and stands between it and the mirror. He and the picture are reflected deeply and with a certain immobility as if the surface that points out the depths were all.

And was the trip a good one?

Yes. Quite good.

The amber light trembles. It is a train on the underground shaking the foundations. The last of the light, as a weak sun goes down somewhere behind Peckham, is hectic in the room.

He moves and the picture resumes its identity, mountain, water, boat and tiny human figure.

As he moves away I see the vase on the table tall with its scarecrow tulips caught in an awful ecstasy of dehydration.

Sorry, he says in that bright graceful way (for he is a small man, much given to detail and high french polish), following my look.

It is not dehydration that has killed them, merely the slow starvation of a thing cut from its root.

I pour the water in the sink and the smell of old bogs, of the sick gasses of primeval stew, comes up to me.

That stinks, he says, wholly without rancour.

I wash it down with clean water.

Unseasonal a flash lights up the sky on the horizon.

That was a big one, he says.

No rumble follows.

The woman straightens up and listens, rubbing the warm patch on her forehead with the very much cooler back of her right hand.

She steps out of the stable and makes sure the door to the shed is shut firmly.

The clouds that lie in layers over to the West have shifted and their shape defines a change in the weather.

Drops fall on her head, three, then two, then after a pause she puts her hand out but the rain has stopped.

She walks quickly towards the house. The wind stirs up towards her and she crosses her arms and clasps the bones of her shoulders.

What fate have I now to decide for her?

Or is the notion of a fate in all this clatter of the mind and world irrelevant?

The light comes on inside the house and on the half-drawn curtain the man's shadow falls.

She hesitates. Her heart beats. I wait as though she held within her hand the seed of me, as though her wish, her thought, the fine hair rising on the skin above her wrist were hieroglyphs that if one could decipher might reveal the self peeled of everything except its own irrevocable strangeness.

Did you hear the thunder?

I shake my head.

But even as I do a sound like fabric tearing comes jagged over the traffic.

She stops outside the door and turns towards me. We contemplate each other for an instant as the night comes down.

The man who is my man or that which the odd label in these latening times pertains to, draws the curtains.

No, he says, no. There's nothing.

And I agree in tones that you might cleave to, the storm is too far away.

VERTIGO

'You ought to have been a ballet dancer,' Maddy said.

I looked at her and thought, yes, a ballet dancer is what I ought to have been. I often think about the things I ought to have been. It is one of my worst habits, thinking about what I ought to have been, rather than about what I am.

'You've got the body,' Maddy said. I looked at her, harder, wondering whether she was joking. Maddy was a great one for making jokes.

'No, I mean –' She stopped and lifted her chin and opened her eyes very wide. She looked like the kind of small, wild creature you imagine surprising in a forest. Quick to alarm, and delicate as it takes flight. Yes, Maddy was very delicate. You thought you might break her. You thought if you caught her around the wrist a little too hard, the bones might crack. I caught her once, around the wrist, like that. The bones didn't crack. But I always thought they might do.

Maddy's delicacy was the most astounding thing about her. She was it and it was she.

'Oh, how *can* I –' she would say, quite often, looking into the mirror and putting the tips of her fingers up to the sides of her face. She made a little *moue* with her lips, as though she were flirting with her own reflection. But it was much more likely, because she so frequently did it, that she was flirting with me.

'Oh, how *can* I –' in that slightly rueful way, mockscandalized, how *can* I be the imperfect-perfect thing the mirror tells me, how *can* I be this carnal creature, aware of the taste of my breath, and the way it feels as it comes out in a rush over the back of my teeth?

Of course I have no idea whether she was really thinking any of these things. But these things are what I thought she was thinking. They are the thoughts her eyes told me were behind her eyes. But eyes can tell you anything. Even your own.

I first noticed just how delicate Maddy was when I saw her walking towards me, quite high up on one of those concrete corridors that seem to suspend themselves from nothing, that you get in English architecture *circa* 1965. It could have been almost anywhere, a housing estate in South London, or a University campus, set inconveniently on the outskirts of some provincial town. It was neither. Maddy walking towards me happened in a place I can only call indescribable. It is indescribable most probably because the place it really happened was in my head.

Maddy walking towards me was like being confronted by a Giacometti sculpture. In the distance she looked tiny and frail, a strip of something with the light behind it. As she got nearer, with that curiously jerky up-and-down movement approaching people have, she began to take on the definite outline that was to attach to itself, very much later, the title 'Maddy'.

There are some people whose outline is more definite than the detail contained within it. Maddy was one of them. I think of Maddy almost always with the light behind her, so that something about her expression remains hidden, so that I am never entirely sure of the nature of her look. Is she looking at me, or past me? That is a question I have never been able satisfactorily to answer. Maddy, looking at me or past me. Maddy, making a little *moue* with her mouth as she flirts with her own reflection in the glass.

I have always been attracted to women of a certain type. The first woman I fell in love with was my grandmother, or, rather, I fell in love with a miniature of my grandmother (who was even then long dead). My grandmother, with her hair piled high and her ears showing, and her neck slender but curiously powerful in a high collar edged with the narrowest strip of lace. My grandmother looked out at me from the slightly curved surface of the miniature as though from the unknown ellipses of another world. Her very distance lent her the elusive charm on which desire is based. It was harmless. I kept the miniature in a velvet box, and took it out very often, and looked at it.

The first time I looked at Maddy I thought of the miniature of my grandmother. It was something about the way Maddy put her hand up to her neck. My grandmother had come alive. I went up to Maddy and said the sort of thing you say at a time like that, but she was waiting for someone and I didn't get very far. It was in a café, one of those artsy cafés you get in university towns, and Maddy looked artsy, with three earrings in one ear and one in the other, and her hair coming over onto the one side and leaving the other side quite exposed, so that you noticed her cheekbone, just below which was a wedge-shaped freckle, it looked odd but at the same time endearing.

Seeing Maddy in the café happened quite a long time after seeing her in my head. Seeing her that first time, suspended, no beginning, no end, that was an experience. It was like going out on the suspension bridge at Clifton, *that* was an experience too. I was about five and my mother took me out onto it, and as I looked down into the ravine beneath it, the gorge, the Cheddar gorge (call it what you will, they've anaesthetized it now with guardrails and tea shops, and a mobile lavatory that plays 'God Save the Queen' when you close the door), as I looked down a funny thing happened. I saw myself far below me. I was a tiny figure, almost identically dressed. It was a minute before I recognized myself. I screamed, and kept on screaming. Someone had to help my mother get me off the bridge. When my mother took me off the bridge she shook me till my teeth rattled. Ever since then, I've been extremely frightened of heights.

All that came back to me, the bridge, my mother, the way my teeth cracked up against one another (and I wet myself too, I think I remember that correctly, going home in the car) when I met Maddy again in the café, and went up and spoke to her, and didn't get very far because she was waiting for friends.

I looked at Maddy and she looked up at me, hunching her shoulder a little as she stirred her coffee, and trailing the tips of her fingers through the rising steam, and I felt something open up, and I took hold of the back of the chair, and saw that she was still looking at me, and I decided then that I didn't like the green colour of her eyes.

It's the detail of a woman that gets you. Overall gorgeousness leaves me cold. It's the detail, the way a hand configures with a wrist, the timing of speech or silence. Sometimes when a woman's lying next to you, a sense of the incredible nature of it goes through you, a sense of the incredible nature of this woman lying next to you, to whom things are done, by you if she wants you to, things no one else has done, or at least, not exactly as you do them, that's what you think at the time, although afterwards you know it isn't so, can't be so, you just need to deceive yourself.

With Maddy in the café I felt the detail begin to insinuate itself into the fabric of my mind, and it disturbed me, I like my mind to be inviolate. Maddy said in answer to my question (I must have asked a question), that no, she couldn't, because she was meeting friends. What was it that I asked her to do? I have absolutely no recollection. Perhaps it was something as harmless as allowing me to join her. It must have been something relatively harmless because she smiled as she shook her head, and I stood for a minute just watching how her hair came forward and went back three or four times, watching it move as her head moved. I am sure, when I think about it properly, that I asked whether I could join her.

We got together. It was a week or two later. It could have been longer than that. All I am sure of is, when I met her in the cafe I had a coat on, with the collar turned up, and when we got together I had on a sweater, and was carrying my books in the crook of my left arm.

Maddy didn't look like a Giacometti sculpture this time. She was much more solid. It is possible (I have discovered) for things to be delicate and solid at the same time. Delicacy – true delicacy – has a core of something indestructible. Maddy was standing at a bus stop looking indestructible. She had on a short, fluffy jacket and her hips and legs came out from below the jacket in a peculiarly inevitable way. Maddy looked inevitable. It was (I realized) inevitable that she should have been standing at the bus stop, and inevitable that I should have seen her there. When I saw her and spoke to her I felt the thing that was like a gap opening up again. We stood there talking for quite a long time and my books felt very heavy in the crook of my left arm. I remember watching Maddy's hands (which I never got to like) and noticing how the tips of her fingers were square, and her palms squarish too. She didn't move her hands very much. I have always liked women who move their hands. It gives me a necessary sense of their transience. But it didn't matter just then, that Maddy didn't move her hands, because the feeling of inevitability had come to both of us and we knew it was just a matter of time before we'd end up in bed.

'Fro' was the first word I saw, written on the mirror in lipstick after Maddy had gone. I lay in the half dark and thought, 'Fro' is the opposite of 'to'. It didn't make any sense. Maddy hadn't written 'Fro', she had written 'with love from Maddy', and the 'm' of the 'from' was hastily written and indistinct.

It wasn't really dark at all. It was daylight, but the curtains were drawn, and the room looked dark and secret, and the bed, and my body in it under the sheets, looked dark and secret too, which was strange, because all of it, to one extent or another belonged to me. But that is how it is sometimes. The things that belong to you are the strangest of all.

I didn't get up straight away but lay there, and the smell of Maddy was in my bed, and it was a light smell, barely there, but a heavy smell too, that carried with it intimations of texture, you felt if you put out your hand you could touch her, and repeat the thick sense of her flesh next to your skin.

'I didn't think, as you sometimes think when a woman has just left you, of what I'd done to her, or she'd done to me, all the things that you do, or don't do, probably, but would like to in some half thought out way that stands between you and it, the doing, like a parable. I thought instead, or perhaps it is truer to say I visualized, because Maddy was there on the back of my eye clad in nothing but light, the way she turned her head and looked at me. In the turn of her head (I thought at that instant) the secret of my existence was revealed. I suppose in that sentiment lies the essence of what some people would refer to as love.

I got out of bed more slowly and consideringly than usual and spent a long time looking at a new bruise on the inside of my thigh that was a strange colour somewhere between red and grey. Further up, my genitals lay along the fold where my belly and leg met, in a little, used-up looking heap. It was odd, odd to see myself in the incomplete way you have to, odd to witness my own irremediable awkwardnesses. I got up and drew back the curtains and the light came in. It was a light half way between city light and country light. It had the density of the former and the clarity of the latter. It made the things in my flat seem very separate from one another, very much individual objects. The colours do not retain, in my memory at least, any element of distinction. It is the shape and definition of everything that renders it, and the moment, monumental. The bed was sculpted and the sheets were folded back onto themselves in waves of stone. The bookcase, which was tall and narrow, stood in the attitude of a sentinel beside the door. The papers on my table, spread out in their usual hurried way, seemed congealed in a sense of yesterday. There was no colour in anything, the light was so strong it drained all the colour into itself. The faint smell of mildew that habitually accompanied my life in that room at that time, had gone.

I wiped the lipstick off the mirror, the letters separately and deliberately, the words so to speak by default, and an unattached little thumb or finger print of lipstick next to the frame, put there carelessly as Maddy grasped and tilted the mirror to the right angle, and adopted (I suppose) her characteristic air of concentration, the eyebrows down over her eyes without actually scowling, a little ridge evident around the edges of her lips. What is it that makes some things lodge in the memory? That brownish thumb or finger print stands like an effigy in the centre of my head. In it are contained what was, what is, and ever will be the sum of that which I construct as 'Maddy'.

Perhaps I should go back to the beginning. But it is very difficult to find a beginning. Perhaps I should go back to the well-dressed little replica of myself who watched himself from a great height and felt the world revolve around him, and felt himself revolve around what he didn't know, you never know, but it's there nevertheless, a grain of something irreducible, lodged in the soft folds at the centre of yourself. Maddy, I suppose, could have put her hand in like a surgeon and removed that grain. And then. Would she have held it up to the light, like a diamond, scrutinized it clinically, estimating its value and worth? Would she have rolled it between thumb and forefinger like a bit of dirt? Would she have cast it off from her with a careless movement, cast me off from her, out into space, on a trajectory not of my own choosing, helpless to determine the nature and pace of my fall?

Maddy. I read her Dylan Thomas on darkish afternoons until I could no longer see the words, so carefully arranged on the page. '*In my craft or sullen art / Exercised in the still night / When only the moon rages.*' I told her I wanted to be a writer. She thought that was romantic. So did I (at the time). '*The lovers, their arms / Round the griefs of the ages.*' How odd it is to be young. How strange (when I think of it now) that gradual loss of light on those apparently limitless winter afternoons.

We drove to see her parents and I declaimed (for most of the way) 'A Refusal to Mourn'. The last line was Maddy's favourite: '*After the first death, there is no other*'.

Her parents welcomed me. They were amiable, ordinary people. Their ordinariness made me feel awkward. I was unused to it. They had never been (so they told me) to Clifton. They had a house half way up a hill, in Herefordshire, overlooking one of the smaller villages. There were no more than thirty houses in the village, and it was unlit still, so that at night when you looked out the roofs in the valley looked ghostly.

I walked out at night with Maddy and told her to do her coat up. It was Spring, or supposed to be, late April, but it was one of those Aprils that stay cold right to the very end. She did her coat up mock-obediently, and put her hand in the bend of my arm, inside the elbow, like older women do with their husbands, a gesture of remembered intimacy, an emblem of passion (perhaps) that existed a long time ago.

I could feel the warmth of Maddy unwinding around her, even through her coat, which was dutifully buttoned up, and through mine, which was open so that the air, which had mist in it, touched my skin through the holes in the centre of the stitches of my woollen jumper. She pressed up against me and said,

'You'll come, later?'

I nodded, and she must have seen me because she didn't say any more. I hadn't wanted to speak. I supposed I couldn't. Sometimes what you want to say just stays there. I didn't say anything, and we stood on the narrow little terrace outside her parents' house, and looked down at what I always thought of afterwards as 'Maddy's valley', that fold in the Herefordshire countryside, holding a little mist in it, holding a lot of darkness, with the lights in the houses all turned out now, and the roofs catching at their edges the merest reflection of sky.

It seems to me that there's a life you lead that happens inside the other life. It's hidden. Quite hidden. Like a circle within a circle. Like a sphere within a sphere. It's in the mind partly, in memory, but not only there. It's the life of what-if. Of all the myriad possibilities, the things you don't do, the things that don't become things. Sometimes it seems that I have lived many lives simultaneously, and yet lived none. At the centre of myself is a well, a bottomless well. Am I the cylinder of darkness, or the shaft of something inexplicable that contains it? These are the questions I come to again and again in my recollections of Maddy. And yet, Maddy was a woman. And yet. In my relation to Maddy, I was a man.

I did not go to Maddy's room that night. She came to mine. I made love to her very quietly, it was quite late, about one o'clock in the morning, and everything was very quiet, and her parents were finally settled in bed. Her parents knew, I could tell when I next saw them, and I didn't like the fact. I didn't like the fact of the previous night with Maddy revisited in their eyes.

The next night, when Maddy said from somewhere quite close to me in the darkness,

'What is it?'

I didn't reply. When I didn't reply she kissed my shoulder (her lips were rather wet and I wiped the wet shape of them off almost at once) and then she got up very lightly and soundlessly, and went back to her own room.

Gravestones have always held for me a particular fascination. I know I am not alone in this. But one's fascinations seem, at the time of experiencing them, unique.

Maddy took me to the churchyard where her ancestors were buried.

'You see?' she said, pushing aside a large branch of ivy. It was before churchyards had fallen prey to the mania for tidyness that has spoiled almost all of them. We paused by a very worn gravestone, leaning over at an angle, very grey and plain and solid, with lichen growing for decoration in tiny, fanlike scallops along a crack.

'Great-great-grandfather Amos,' Maddy said. She folded her hands in front of her and stood with her ankles together. I deciphered the name with difficulty, and beneath it '*Sarah, Wife of the Above*'.

I have read somewhere that there are only twenty-five generations between me and Jesus. I felt, looking at the angle of Great-great-grandfather Amos's gravestone, that it might be true.

I felt other things too, standing by Maddy with her ankles together and a wind coming round the corner of the church and laying the grasses that grew up quite tall by Amos's gravestone over onto their sides. I felt as though the whole world was in movement. Everything pivoted on the axis of Amos's grave. Can you understand the exhilaration and the terror that such a shifting sense of things brings? I do not know now, quite, whether I understand it myself. In the hedges and the bushes, the leaves were showing their undersides. The fields tilted, then re-arranged themselves slowly and carefully until everything was in order, right up to the far ones lost in the blur that ends quite suddenly in the horizon line. I kissed Maddy and her lips were warmer than I had expected.

I have a memory which seems to be nothing to do with any of this but which is, in some strange way, fundamental. I have a picture in my head which I take out and look at sometimes and put back carefully, much as one may an emblem of another way of being, a campaign medal, a silver snuff box, a pair of impossibly tiny-fingered satin gloves. Really, there are two pictures. One dark, one light. One day, one night. One is a dream, perhaps. A dream within a dream. Both images are of my mother.

I am a small boy. A child with legs that come out of the cuffs of his trousers and hands that protrude in bunches from the ends of the stuff of his arms. I do not know when, exactly. Perhaps it is after we have come back from Clifton. Perhaps it is entirely another time. It is cold, I know that, colder in some strange way than it is possible to be on this earth. I wake up in the middle of the night, one of those very long nights that mark, like milestones, the interstices of childhood. I wake up and sense that I exist only in space, that there is nothing behind or below or around me, that there will never be, that I am condemned to this limitless existence, trapped in the endless destiny of the drop. I wake up and know there is nothing, and the knowledge is big inside me like a bubble expanding, and I have to touch her before the edges of the bubble reach my edges, and I become nothing. I have to touch her and I put my hand out, and her arm when I touch it is nothing, no flesh, no substance, my mother has already become a ghost.

Then in daylight, standing at the corner of the house with her hair blowing over her face, strings of it, whipping at her earlobes.

'The wind, the wind,' she says, hearing it come from somewhere very far away. And her knuckles are pointed as she clasps her arms tightly around her, and the ends of her fingers disappear into her own flesh.

I think that sex and death are indivisible, two kinds of isolation, in both of which the ephemeral and the eternal fuse. That was the thought that came to me when I kissed Maddy and her lips were warmer than I had expected, after she had showed me the graves of her ancestors, three hundred years of inter-relation, displayed in that untidy churchyard, made flesh in the sweep of her hand.

I think very often of those tilting gravestones, still under the moving branches of the yew, sinking (in my imagination) out of sight as I get into the car with Maddy, who looks over her shoulder as we drive away. The incident is like a tiny hieroglyph scratched on the fabric of my mind with the tip of a pin.

Maddy did not come to my room the following night. I do not think that I ever afterwards made love to her. She had turned (I do not know how it was) into an idea. I lay in the dark and thought of her, and the thought dissolved into nothing. She existed as music exists. She had become (in some way I do not fully understand) an illusion.

I had left the window open, because it had got warmer suddenly, in the way it can do in April, and there was a rushing sound, faintly, the stream probably, that ran at the far end of her parents' orchard and in which (they told me) later in the Summer you would find trout. I wanted the rushing to stop. I lay there, awake yet not awake, and another picture came to me, the only time it has ever come, of my mother with her hair spread out on the pillow in a star shape, spread out in points as though she had arranged it that way.

'*Promise me*,' she says.

I stand a long way from her but her breath makes the air in the room move. A strange smell mixes in with the perennial smell of antiseptic. It is the peculiar, gassy intimation of impending death.

'*Promise me*,' she says.

I stare into the darkness. The rushing sound has stopped. I think that only memory has the power of resurrection. I think that there are, after all, more than twenty-five generations between me and Christ.

'You ought to have been a ballet dancer,' Maddy said. She laughed as she said it, showing the little ridges in her teeth. She tucked her hand in the crook of my arm, at the elbow. I smelled her scent, faintly, mixed in with the metallic smell you always get outside the National Gallery, in winter anyway, when it gets to be afternoon. We'd been to see a Bacon exhibition and I think the laughter was, in part at least, a necessary reaction. And then, we had recently been happy after a fashion, and I suppose the laughter too was a reflection of that.

'Rothbart,' I said, not without irony. 'I've always liked women who wear black.'

Although it was very cold the fountains in the Square were, unaccountably, still working. Before it froze, I thought, someone would turn them off.

'Have you a five?' Maddy said. I gave her one. She leaned forward and spun the coin up into the air, and we both watched the grey light fail to catch it on the short parabola before it disappeared end-on into the foam.

Across the city, a clock started to chime.

'Wish!' Maddy said. Her mouth moved, but the fountain drowned out the sound.

'Wish!' Maddy said, and took her hand out of the crook of my arm. The clock was still chiming, it had been joined by other clocks, note after note forming and reforming an intricate pattern of sound. The traffic revved up ready for the lights to change. I said,

'Maddy,' and held out my hand towards her. But she had crossed already and was running up the steps ahead of me, her ankles brittle looking and her shoulders square against the light. The stuff of her skirt, a rather short skirt of pleats that at certain times the light shone through, swayed to the left then to the right. By the time she had reached the top she was tiny and insubstantial, a being in miniature, only half the height of my hand.

I called out 'Maddy' again, but she was too far away to hear me.

My hand will remain, I suppose, fixed in its gesture of supplication, the fingers trailing vapour, the air rare around it and unbreathable, the water in the fountain condemned perpetually to flow. Maddy in outline, high, high above me, an identically dressed little figure, looking down.

Living Memory

The ring when you took it out had lights that came in and out of the stones like a fire had been lit on the far side of them. You closed your eyes tight for a second against it. Then you opened them again and it was there in his hand like you didn't know what precisely, an offering, a recompense, a gift that had its own aspect, retribution maybe, its own way of saying for ever and ever, there, you poor little quick string of a thing, I told you so.

It lay in his hand and she wanted to dash the hand away behind that held it.

His cuff was a little too long and the cufflink an overly noticeable blue.

I am here, she thought, with these past things like statues.

There had been a story once, of a garden of statues that had come to life.

Well, if all *that* lot came to life, what an odd sort of occurrence it would be.

A moment only had passed and he cleared his throat to recall himself to her attention.

The small-town noises outside the window came in.

She thought to herself, God, this is how it could be, today and all days. And maybe even married to a man like that.

Who cared about politics? The only politics she knew was the look that passed between people.

What a look it *was*. What it could do. In that look was contained the whole of creation.

He closed his fingers round the ring and put it back down in the box which had a little knob on the front that you pressed, and was made of grey crocodile leather.

There was a crown on the top of the box which meant, she supposed, the jeweller was by Royal Appointment.

Flo was like that and always had been.

It had come about because her father, who was known as Great Uncle Johnny, had come down with Syph.

He'd got it out in the East where he'd been something big in the East India Company. They'd paid him off with a cheque for fifty thousand.

That was quite a sum when you thought about it, or would be nowadays.

He'd come back and married Florence's mamma, who was a widow. Florence had remembered it. She'd had quite a thing, as a child, for Uncle Johnny. She'd never talked all that much about later, when the long time of it not showing was over, and Uncle Johnny had taken to his bed, or had been made to, and bits of him dropped off, his nose went first if she remembered rightly, and then one by one the pink tips of his fingers.

It was no surprise the way he died, with Florence outside the door with her arms crossed over the front of her and clasping her shoulders.

He'd died, according to Florence whose top lip shook a bit when she spoke of it, cursing the God that made him and the name of his fate.

All that was long ago and far removed, perhaps, from the room in the town with the man with the ring in his hand.

But oh it seemed to her to be so much part of the same question.

The stone in the hand with the fingers that shut out the fire was the point of it.

All roads that came and went here intersected.

If you were a scientist it would be like you had come upon the moment of supreme discovery.

The man with the overly blue cufflinks hemmed at her again.

The reading of a will was, in the days Uncle Johnny was a product of and, to a lesser extent Florence herself, a formal thing.

She had decided not to wear her jeans as a token of respect to this older way of being. She had on a skirt, a latter day version of what

Florence would have worn but more fashionable.

Whatever it was she wore, Florence had never thought much of it. It was no doubt an aspect of her very great attachment. Love moved like God did, in a way that was mysterious.

And what was it?

Related no doubt to this sense of a great big gap that was absence.

It was like leaning over the edge of a cliff and being thankful, then finding yourself falling on down through the air.

There are certain other items, he said with his mouth pursed up, and some are quite valuable.

She did not care a thing for any other object but the one that was in the box that he would shortly hand her.

I am a woman of property, the voice would go on saying right inside her.

But she had been that for a long time.

She stepped out into the street and the sun came at her like a white band over the top of the Post Office.

The top had used to be higher, when she was a child, but there had been a fire in the night, one very dark night in nineteen sixty-three.

She had seen from the hill the flames and they had looked like paper. There was about fire from a distance always the aspect of an animated toy.

She had hurried down late to catch the eight o'clock bus which still went then, and when she got home had told Flo about it.

The next day there had been the building with no top on. Its fine turrets were all gone.

And when they had built it back up again which they decided to because it was a historic building and such things needed to be pre-served, in one form or another, they had left the turrets off because of the cost.

Ever since then it had had an odd, squat appearance.

And all the new people who came to the town never knew what it had looked like before.

It was an insidious kind of corruption.

Sic transit gloria, Flo said.

It was either that night, or the night Kennedy died which was in the same November, that Flo showed her the ring and said it would be corning to her.

It was difficult to take in what that meant.

The room was lit by two lamps that cast their opposing shadows.

Outside the wind went *tic-tic* and the darkness filled up the comers of the garden.

You could almost see how the darkness would settle like a coating on the sharp part at the edge of each blade of grass.

Yours, Flo said, with the ring on fire in the dip in her hand that the lines went into.

After I am gone.

Gone had a very final sound to it that could not have meaning to one not yet accustomed to the notion of finality.

The years with all their myths and their accoutrements had passed.

Flo fell in love very quietly at the edge of one's consciousness and fell out of it again.

It is true that when you go back to a place the trees are taller.

The photograph of Uncle Johnny that had been put away came out again.

Flo put things in order.

Then she herself fell in love and time ceased to have meaning. What is the nature of one spring or another when you are aware, you think, only of eternal want?

But then the notion of eternity itself dissolves in the gap between touches.

She came back to herself.

Who is this old woman with the joints of her knuckles up like a frightened spider?

It had not happened as quickly as that, or at least, only in one sense of the happening.

Many things had occurred.

There were the big things that marked your life like signposts, or were supposed to.

They seemed to her conversely very small when she thought of them.

There were the small ordinary things that filled up every day that you could never remember.

A whole life might be spent in trying to remember such things. A life was a very short thing indeed and it was a pity to waste it.

What then were the things that had significance?

What gave your life significance was the pattern of images of things.

The night Kennedy died which might or might not have been the night of the fire, when she thought about it afterwards it was, she came to the conclusion, a week before or a week after, precise sequence never mattered in events; the night Kennedy died Flo had said,

I am going to make my will.

How odd it was to think of a will as something to be made rather than your own self in a curious way enacted.

Everything you *did* was nothing, if there would come a point where you could no longer do it.

The ring would be hers, and the other rings, and the pictures, and the regency dining chairs, and the carved Tudor chest with the secret drawer that somebody's famous papers had been hidden in, some-body famous himself that had escaped from a Castle in one of the times that was troubled, when men wanted more things than they had a right to, women too, it was an odd facet of being human that you always wanted, when you got down to it, more than you had.

The ring that she meant wasn't the fine hoop of sapphires with the gold scrollwork wrought so deftly on the side. Nor was it even the boat-shaped file of diamonds with the little goldtipped claws that held the stones, so brilliant-cut and winking, in their place. It was not of course the gold band wrought like a belt with the two not quite matched amethysts, her birth stone and something she'd never been overly fond of, something about it reminded her of the drunks she'd seen in the streets, more of them now than had been, with the bottles tipped up to their lips and the same coloured liquid going down into their system to rot out the guts and the lungs.

The ring that Florence had meant and that sat in her palm like it had in his aflame in a way that flames never were in the world, or at least not this one, was the ring with the perfect opals all three in a row with the two pairs of diamonds between them, a bit flashy no doubt by some worldly standards but magical, you could imagine when you looked down into the fire in those stones Vesuvius erupting. Yes. That was what you could imagine. Vesuvius erupting, and after, the destruction of the world.

Now there begins, she thought, walking along the street away from the post office with the sun in a slab left behind her on the pavement, the remaking.

Kennedy had died and they had listened to the news of it coming on the wireless.

She had cried.

What a pity it was, Florence said, and the man so handsome.

Do not ask, my fellow citizens, what America can do for you. Ask, rather, what you can do for America.

Oh God, he *was* beautiful, and the way his hair came forward would remain with you.

Ich bin ein Berliner!

And even afterwards, when you took your O-level German, you knew it was a lie.

Ich bin was not a static thing that you could lay your hands on.

No thing was there that you could lay your hands on, not past, not present, not future, not he, not she, not speech, not silence, not even the beginning nor the end of the world.

They were knocking down the frontage of where the old Doctor's had been, that had come once a week with his bag in his hand, but had retired by the time Flo needed him, and the senior partner now was a much too young man and one you couldn't have confidence in, so Flo said, looking sideways out of the window with the grass all flat to her gaze that had been laid out sideways by the wind.

A great big thing like a ball on the end of a chain went *whock!* as it hit right into the building.

She had fallen down and cut her hand around the time that Kennedy had died and Flo had brought her there and the old Doctor had nodded and sent her off for stitches.

The scar where they'd done them up at the local hospital was white on the side of her wrist.

She remembered the Doctor nodding.

It was another doctor entirely that had come out of Flo's room a fortnight ago with a shake of his head.

In her pocket was the box with the ring in that banged against the side of her as she walked.

Flo *was.*

Flo *was not.*

Whock! went the ball on the chain and another bit of the old wall crumbled.

Dust rose.

Machinery that was like the screech of a conveyer belt started. When she had flown in from Paris she thought,

This is a different world.

There was a lot of water in the bottom of the hole that they'd dug that they lowered Flo down into.

So close she could have touched it, with the rain running down the side of the burnished name plate and the ground so like a quagmire the undertaker had caught hold of her arm.

*

When she woke up there was a pigeon hoo-hooing outside the window like when she was a child.

If you saw the pigeon it looked fat with its feathers all out around it.

Something should happen.

There should be an incident.

She got up.

The woman whose name she had forgotten or perhaps she did not know it yet came in to clean.

It seemed to her that the incidents in your life had nothing to do with you.

The evening before she had gone to the glass cabinet with the very particular porcelain plates in and the ivory fan with its wonderful sheaf of green feathers, the tail of some unfortunate long-gone bird, and taken out the old off pair of embroidered slippers, Flo had always said she didn't know who they belonged to, Uncle Johnny'd brought them back with him as a curiosity.

She had asked the question many times when she was a child. And who did the slippers belong to?

The shape of the foot that a used shoe always has was there in the fabric.

And Florence had always answered, in precisely the same tone of voice,

I do not know.

She sat with the old red damask fabric in her hand and the light from the fire flickering.

She had said to the woman, Will you light a fire? although it was April and had been, with the exception of the day in question, unseasonably hot.

The woman had lit the fire in a very business-like way that said, *You are a person who is used to having things done for you.*

The important thing according to Uncle Johnny, Flo had said to her, is the habit of command.

The slippers had about them the very old untouched smell of another world.

Johnny had brought them back and they had lain with the fan and the porcelain behind glass.

There was a photograph of Johnny looking portly, with a stand-up collar.

Flo had fallen passionately in love at the age of eighteen. It was impossible to say what had become of that.

She had never married.

The trap came by clip-clop, clip clop.

We would go on the train to Aunt Evelyn's at Symonds Yat and it took half an hour.

There was a man there once that stepped out from behind a bush with no clothes on and I said to him,

'What on earth d'you think you're doing?'

And then poor Evie's husband died that hanged himself out in the barn with a rope from the rafters.

There was a very good harvest in one of the hot summers after the war.

We hadn't the vote of course, but I'm not sure we were any the worse for it.

And then that Labour lot got in, Ramsay MacDonald, he was a little tout.

And then one day we blackened our eyelashes with a bit of burnt cork and it rained and the black ran down our faces and Mamma said it was a scandal, what young girls were coming to.

Once, there was a murder in the town. It must have been in nineteen hundred and twelve. It was in all the papers. The man was called Hodgson, or Hodgkins. He was engaged to a girl that led him on and it got too much for him. Well, one day of course she threw him over. He followed her home from her mother's that night on the path that went by the river and just when the mist was coming up out of the water, like I don't know what that mist is, when it comes, he strangled her.

Those were the days when the Judge came down once a month for Assizes.

Very fine indeed it was, the Judge in all his robes, and all the other ones I forget the name of, very stately, proceeding up the town.

Assize days and Market days the pubs stayed open.

Your Great Aunt Evie's husband's brother ran a pub, but we don''t talk of it.

Old Scoder-Robinson, he was a dirty old swine, with a string of bastards.

I heard tell (though you never know exactly what it is you should credit) that before he put on his robes on Assize day he'd hire a whore called Monkey Mo for a shilling.

You come back to yourself with the fire flickering.

Put down the slippers.

That old red damask has a flabby feel. Take the ring out of the box and look at it.

Were ever such opals got up out of the surface of the world? Yet you can make them inert just by an angle.

Blue lumps of dull stuff.

The night Kennedy died, which was the night of the fire, or a week before or a week after, the precise sequence of events is never of importance, I cried, and Flo put her arm around me.

Her touch was something I never sought or got used to. There are more things in the world than that, she said. The next day the papers all came out and there were pictures of it.

Flo and I sat down to dinner.

It was a dark and, if I remember rightly, a wild enough night. Flo got out the ring and said it would be coming to me. She put it on my next from smallest finger and it turned around.

She said I would most certainly grow into it.

It seemed to me quite strange that I would ever have fingers that were big enough.

When she had put the ring back in its pale grey crocodile box with the crown on I asked her, more for form's sake than for anything, who the slippers had belonged to.

She said (although I make it up most probably, as something that will round the world as stages do that make the progress of a fable) that those old slippers had belonged to Johnny's servant-mistress, that he had taken to himself at first for pleasure on a trip to Rangoon, and then found, which is always the danger, that she had become more to him than his life.

When the wind comes up in this old house there is a little moaning sound as it comes under the door.

When I was much younger I would say to Flo that it was ghosts rattling the handle.

It is my house now.

There is a letter from the lawyer that confirms my property and my position.

Tomorrow on the plane I will assume myself again.

Tonight what was and is are one and me entirely.

Dearest —.

There are letters to be sent but many will have no recipient.

I take the ring out of the box and notice that one of the opals has a crack in it.

Opals are, it is a well known fact, unlucky.

When he cursed his maker and his fate did Uncle Johnny have the faintest sense of how the flesh had been of her his servant-mistress in a Rangoon that was steamy?

Kennedy went all swiftly with the blood out round him, in a blur.

I put the ring onto my next to smallest finger and the flames light up how perfectly it sits upon my hand.

Outside the rain is coming down and now I hear it.

Almost you could think of knuckles tapping up against the pane.

I smooth the slippers down the way of the nap and put them in the cabinet.

The green feathers lift a little in the draught from my hand then settle.

The room adjusts itself around them like an adjunct to a space.

Breathe in the bright humidity, the scents of narrow alleys with their sudden shutting out of light.

A woman turns, goes to the door, hesitates.

I take her hand and step out with her onto the dark surface of the world.

ACKNOWLEDGEMENTS

Acknowledgements are due to the editors of the following publications where some of these stories first appeared. 'Losing' and 'Charity' appeared in *Planet*. 'Losing' also appeared in *The Green Bridge* (Seren, 1988) and *The New Penguin Book of Welsh Short Stories* (1993). 'L'Hotel des Grands Hommes' appeared in *Prism, New Writing 1* (Minerva/British Council, 1992), *The Works* (WUW, 1990) and *Classworks* (Hodder, 1996). 'Charity' and 'A Place in Wales' appeared *Luminous and Forlorn* (Honno, 1994). 'Fencing' appeared in *The Word Party* (UEA, 1991).

THE AUTHOR

Clare Morgan is a fiction writer and literary critic who lives in Gwynedd and Oxford. Her novel *A Book for All and None* was published by Weidenfeld & Nicolson and her short story collection, *An Affair of the Heart*, by Seren. Her stories have been widely anthologized, and broadcast on BBC Radio 4. Her book *What Poetry Brings to Business* was published by University of Michigan Press and her recent writing on the subject has featured in the *Wall Street Journal*, *FastCompany*, and *Humanizing Business: What Humanities can say to Business.* She is founder and director of Oxford University's creative writing degree, and a Fellow of Kellogg College, Oxford.

SCAR TISSUE

In a world of uncertainties, how do human beings navigate the increasingly complex interrelations of love, desire, home, community? Each of the twelve stories in *Scar Tissue* offers a fresh perspective on the nature of individual existence in all its transient vulnerability. From deep country on the Welsh borders to the metropolitan precincts of London or Paris; from the forests of Scandinavia to neatly clapboarded New England; from a Spanish *finca* to Dulles airport; and from the steamy environs of Mumbai to the cooler spaces of a medieval farmhouse in Snowdonia – all these disparate realms intersect with the perennial human need to belong and the impossibility of doing so. The irreducibility of time acts as a continuo throughout the narratives and links loss with longing, hope with love and reveals the tentacular hold the past can have on all present aims and imperatives.

In these lyrical, evocative and searching stories, *Scar Tissue* unflinchingly explores the darker and more challenging aspects of emotional, sexual and familial relationships, while simultaneously celebrating the joys of being alive in an unfathomable world.

www.serenbooks.com